DATE DUE

THE DEATH
OF JOE GILEAD

**Center Point
Large Print**

**This Large Print Book carries the
Seal of Approval of N.A.V.H.**

THE DEATH
OF JOE GILEAD

William A. Luckey

CENTER POINT PUBLISHING
THORNDIKE, MAINE

To MML and RGL

This Center Point Large Print edition
is published in the year 2006 by arrangement with
Golden West Literary Agency.

Copyright © 1987 by William A. Luckey.

The text of this Large Print edition is unabridged. In other
aspects, this book may vary from the original edition. Printed in
Thailand. Set in 16-point Times New Roman type.

ISBN: 1-58547-859-8
ISBN 13: 978-1-58547-859-0

Library of Congress Cataloging-in-Publication Data

Luckey, William A.
    The death of Joe Gilead / William A. Luckey.--Center Point large print ed.
    p. cm.
    ISBN 1-58547-859-8 (lib. bdg. : alk. paper)
    1. Large type books. I. Title.

PS3562.U2548D43 2006
813'.54--dc22

2006015905

Prologue

"Good night, Evan. Come to bed soon." The old man nodded, even though she could not see him in the darkness. He could hear her footsteps take the stairs at a halting pace, resting every second step. Then there would be a long silence, followed by the soft closing of the bedroom door.

He could imagine the routine: the release of the long white hair, the thin body uncovered then shielded by the blue checked flannel gown that would cover the gaunt frame. Finally she would turn to the high roped bed, pull back the yellow star quilt, and climb into the coldness of bleached muslin sheets.

She would be thinking that she needed him to warm the damp bedding, that she needed his hand on hers to find sleep.

But he could not sleep. The past two years sleep had come less and less easily. A face would come between him and healthy sleep, a mocking face that grew older and thinner and more distant without him knowing. A face that seared inside his eyelids and woke him trembling and wet.

He reached out to the oil lamp beside the high rocker, and the small movement woke the devils living in him, brought the ceaseless pain to remind him of bones broken, muscles strained going back thirty years. He looked at the hand reaching out in the dim light—his hand; spotted now with dark stains, fingers blunted, knuckles spread. A toll paid to his work—a rope from a running horse, barbed-wire mended fence, stringing new lines, building a new barn. Two fingernails on the right hand were gone, torn out by a cloven hoof when the grulla mare went down under a stampeding herd. The fingertips were still tender, even after years of rasping wear on leather and wood. The left hand flexed slowly, bringing a grimace to the lined and seamed face. The thumb had an awkward set; the ring finger was missing the tip, leaving a twisted nail and flattened pad.

Evan Gilead touched the knob at the base of the glass shade. The light flared too brightly, and he cursed. It was a new lamp, to replace the one he'd knocked over last month. His dark eyes smarted, and the shadowed light caught the lines and hollows of his face.

It had been a handsome face, strong-planed and fine, with eyes set wide apart and clear under a ridged brow. The nose was long and hooked, miraculously unbroken through the years, arched over the heavy upper lip now wrinkled and drawn in over fewer teeth and loosened muscle. There had been a heft and a strength to the old man that stayed with him, that left him wide-shouldered and deep through the chest, but now carried a sag to let puffy flesh rest on the wide belt buckle, almost obscuring its silver in the folded body.

He stayed in the chair, head lowered, eyes watching the floor as if to question the first step. He was permanently bent over now, from a year past when the mismatched team had tipped the wagon and caught him underneath. The doc had told him something was cracked near the spine, not just the ribs at his side but something the doc's quick fingers and time could not heal. . . .

Evan could almost hear the bed above him creak as his wife gave in to sleep. The bed had come west with them, along with the perfection of the square walnut dresser, the bulk of the high wardrobe that had been her dowry. His promise to her had been his youth, his unquenchable belief in his power and strength, his rightness. Together they'd built this ranch out of the harsh and unending swell of the Dakota territory. It was here they'd chosen to spend their life together and to raise their family.

The old man leaned forward and then stood up. There was enough light for him to find the cane without fumbling. He could go nowhere without his cane. The smooth heavy knob fitted easily in his hands, as if it had been waiting for him all its life.

He coughed and snorted, took several steps in the black, and found the familiarity of the solid chair to the right of the fireplace. Beyond the chair was a small table, then the doorway to the kitchen. But if he turned left, he would touch the base of the stairway that would take him to the sleeping woman and the soft agony of long waking hours in the high bed.

An urge took him through the kitchen to the back door, to the harsh and waiting night.

The door opened too slowly. Heavy wood, ponderous and safe against intruders, the door swung without squeaking, yielding the cold night air to the old man. He tasted the air, smelled the dusting of snow that chilled the early spring buds.

Evan could no longer look to the rim of the bluff and beyond, could no longer see the stars overhead or the thin sliver of moon. The broad edge of the bluff was his protection, his measure of safety from wind and snow, the bursts of spring and summer storms. The high wall eased and flattened farther down the valley, leveling to meet the rise of land near a small stream. But here the bluff reared high and wild, offering its protection.

But the bluff and its unyielding bulk had not been able to save the family. And the big house was denied the generations that a man and a woman had produced, for the big house and the protected ranch were empty. There were only the two old Gileads, whose cautious steps and soft talk mocked the unheard sounds of running children and laughter, of the love between strong men and willing women.

There had been a family. William MacGregor Gilead, dead almost twenty-five years. Died a child at fifteen, spilled under a chunky sorrel down a narrow canyon. And Margaret Elizabeth, four years old, burned with a fever, lying beside two unmarked graves, two unnamed children stillborn and buried in a short day.

There was one more grave on the bluff. The grave of a full grown man. The betraying wetness came to the old eyes, and Evan Gilead cursed his weakness. Henry Johnson Gilead, dead and buried nine years past. Murdered. By his own brother.

The old man shuddered and blamed the cold. He would never sleep tonight. Behind his closed eyes was the memory that tore into him. The face of their youngest child, the blaze of wide green eyes, blood spilled down the torn shirtfront and dried to rusted stains on manacled hands. Blood spotting the faded blue of the denim pants.

He would not form the name, and a fear trembled through his hands, making the tip of the cane rattle on the loose planking. That boy was gone from them, gone forever. Turned out of prison and gone down the trail, beyond the reach of his family.

A good boy, the best of the lot. Straight and lean like his mother, a thinker and a dreamer, a quiet touch with the stock, long hands that eased instinctive fears and soothed irritations. Awed by his older brother, determined to run with him and his bunch. And destroyed by one night of fury.

Bitter memory jabbed the old man, digging under his remaining resolve. Water shimmered in the faded eyes and promised to spill over and run down the seamed face, to expose the shameful tears to the icy cold nighttime air.

The boy had to come home. Had to come back. The hope stayed with Evan, buried inside under the days and the worry.

Chapter 1

Even under the late dusting of snow the land was barren and unending, with only tips of browned grass showing through the soft white. A man had to earn the beauty of this land, the miles of rich graze, the close stands of willow and cottonwoods that hugged the few rivers, the sudden wide valleys and deep gullies.

Joe Gilead knew the land. He'd ridden the miles of grasslands, choused out half-wild cattle from the slanted hills and brush-filled hollows. A long nine years past, this corner of the Dakotas had been his home. He wondered how much the land had changed. And the people living on it.

A flood of memories brought him out of the saddle, then he fought down the eagerness and settled back to the hard comfort of the high cantle and chopped swell, easing his shoulders in the restriction of the heavy wool coat. The horse picked an unfamiliar path down the brush-strewn hill, overcautious on the rocky ground.

Joe knew. Around the bottom of the hill, hidden in the length of a narrow valley, lay the sprawling collection of buildings that was the ranch. It had been his home. A long time ago.

The knot in his belly drove the breath from him. Down below were his parents, and up on the opposite high bluff the silent graves of his brothers and sisters. He had put off this day for two years, but the need to know had finally forced him to saddle the high withered roan and ride from the company ranch in Idaho as winter softened its hold.

The ride in had been long and silent, but he had to know. He knew about his mother, knew she would cry and reach out to hold him, to touch his face. But it was the old man he had to see.

The roan snorted and jumped the last step to the worn trail. Joe shoved the knot back in the hole above his belt and gigged the tired horse into a lope. He wanted to reach the house quickly, have his say, and be gone.

The old house looked no different; the low-slung roof of the veranda shadowed the front of the house. The walls were tight, the high steps to the front door solid and secure. The pale yellow rawness of a new post stood out among the silvered pillars that lined the house.

Joe rode a straight line across the dirt yard. The main barn was snug, doors hung level. The fence line was laced with fresh-cut poles.

A new shed almost hid the lopsided back barn, the first barn the young Gileads had built. Joe rode from habit to that barn, where he and Hank had always kept their mounts, where winter hay was stored.

As he loosened his feet from the wide stirrups, the old door squealed open and a heavy man walked out to stand at the roan's chest. He was a stranger to Joe, a big man well in his thirties, packing a lot of meat on a six-foot frame. Joe felt the tightness come back to twist at his belly.

The dark-haired man spoke without bothering to look

11

beyond the horse's wide chest, and his words were hard.

"You. Get. We got no jobs here and no time for grub line riders. On your way out of here. Now."

Joe couldn't hear the sounds coming from the man. The knot had gone to his head, swelling and pushing away the crispness of the day. He dismounted from the roan, working at bringing moisture to his mouth, wanting to free the words jammed in his throat.

Joe touched ground lightly, steadied himself on the saddle swell, and looked across the horse's neck to the solid wall of the man standing there. Waiting. There was a familiarity to the man he could not place. Then his eyes left the dark stare, and the knot inside him grew, dulling the well-honed instincts that had kept him alive.

The words came to him: "I came to see the Gileads. The mister and his wife. Just want to put up my horse and see them."

He didn't watch the man. He was close enough almost to touch the smoothed and worn wooden latch of the barn door. The heavy pegs holding the wood door together had been bolstered by bent iron nails, and one board had been shattered, the rotted ends a pale orange.

He led the roan gelding one step, forcing the horse past the dark-haired man. Joe could see inside the barn, could count the empty stalls, smell the last of the dried grass fed out during the winter freeze.

The blue head was jerked from his hold. Joe ducked at the blurred swing of the meaty fist as the blow caught him along his jaw, slamming him against the spooked horse. Another blow under his wishbone sent him under shuffling horse's hooves. The horse panicked and kicked out.

Joe did not see the heavy man pull the horse over him and send it inside the dark barn. He lay in the soggy, snow-dampened dirt, fighting for his breath.

There was a brutal pleasure behind the words: "I warned you, bud. We got no handouts for the likes of you, and there ain't nothing a saddle bum like you got that's worth bothering them old folks. Now you get up and take your licking. It'll remind you to stay the hell away from the Three V."

There was a surprising chuckle from the grim face. "I'll leave you well enough to ride, but that's all you get."

Joe staggered to his feet, feigning battered confusion. He blocked the expected blow with his left arm and drove his fist into the wide exposed belly of the man.

A fist connected to Joe's face that split his cheek and sent him struggling to keep his feet. There was a brief moment, when the big man stepped back, did not press the fight, when the two men measured each other.

Joe saw the misshapen ear, the network of tiny scars above both eyes, the nose spread wide and flattened at the tip. The man was a brawler. And whatever the man saw when he sized up Joe enlarged his grin.

The trickle of blood that ran down Joe's face and stained his faded coat enraged him. He sidestepped back and tipped his shoulder to draw the big man to

13

him. Then he slid by the short, reaching fist to land three quick blows to the man's belly. He ducked and spun again, knowing to stay away from the ponderous bulk. But not before an unseen fist drove him to his knees, doubling a fire in his gut. A boot toe caught Joe under his ribs and twisted him on his back. He could see the shape of the big man above him, hear the words through the ringing in his ears.

"Ain't so much now, buster. I told you to get and you'll get. Strapped across that bronc's back and out of here backassed."

The grin was a torment. Joe rolled on top of the big man and came down to drive the end of the words from his opponent's mouth, as their two bodies hit the churned ground. Seven years of schooling had taught Joe the rules of this fight.

He butted his head over and over in the man's face, sending a shower of blood over them both. His knee came up into the man's groin as thick arms pounded up and down his back. Teeth caught his ear, and Joe swung his head wildly, jamming his forehead into the mangled nose.

Then the hammering fists found his lower back and pounded hard, darkened his vision, blurring his sight, slowing his efforts. Survival kept him battering at the bloody face even when he could no longer see through blackness.

One more blow to his unprotected back froze Joe in the pain. He slumped over the mountainous body, and the man below him shrugged the limp body off his massive chest, to lie facedown in the new mud.

The big man staggered to his knees and remained there for a long second, swaying slightly. Then he rose to his feet to look down at the long, still form of the saddle bum. A brief flint of unwanted admiration showed in the dark eyes, then disappeared as the man watched Joe's struggle to move.

Neither man was aware of the commotion in the ranch yard, the running feet, a high, shrill scream. They knew only the challenge of each other.

Joe stood on widespread feet and found the support of the old barn at his back. A shake of his head brought a quick clean pain to dissolve the mist. With no thought he lurched forward at the wavering figure of the enemy, focused on the wide shoulders and leering eyes too close to him.

Where was the son of a . . . A hand at his neck pulled him upright, spun him around, held him in a vise. A fist drove into his unprotected face, and Joe feebly raised his hands. A laugh came with another blow that split Joe's brow, the next blow widened the opened cheek, the next tore his mouth against loosened teeth. Joe Gilead crumpled into the dirt at the feet of his grinning challenger.

Ed Duncan's mind finally registered the sounds coming up behind him. Too bad the missus was home to see this one. He poked the body with his toe. Nothing. Good goddamn. The bloody man at his feet was outweighed by forty pounds easy, no match for Ed Duncan, yet the son had fought to the end. Duncan grinned through his own blood; he prized that in a man.

It sure enough was the old lady's voice. She'd been complaining enough to Stratmeyer about the violence. And the old man was angry that these line riders were turned away with nothing. But Stratmeyer stayed strict about the rule, and Duncan got to turn the men away.

But most of them didn't fight back like this sucker. Duncan shook his head. Sweat had pooled at his shirt collar and chilled him in the early spring sun. His breath came in deep gasps, each time reminding him the son had gotten in some heavy blows. Ed looked down again, prodded the flattened boy one more time. There was no reaction to his searching boot, no muddy groan, no stirring protest against reawakening pain.

Elissa Stratmeyer reached the back barn first. She pulled up her heavy woolen skirt to run across the muddy yard, and Ed Duncan could see the white layering of petticoats bunched in her hands, shining in the folds of dark green twill.

He wiped again at the sweat and blood covering his face, unconsciously standing straighter against the pull in his groin and chest. He tried to smile at the narrowed eyes but dropped his glance and lowered his head as he saw the fury of the young woman's gaze. Elissa Stratmeyer, Miss Elissa to him, was angry.

Behind the young woman, covering the ground at a much slower pace, came the old man and his wife. The old man was bent over and used a cane to swing his right leg forward, his face watching the ground immediately before him, unable to come upright from the stiffened back. His crablike walk could cover ground fast if needed.

The missus was right behind the old man, towering over him now in her straightness, taller than the husband who had once looked down to her hazel eyes. The strength of will was still there, the rightness, but their bodies had slowed, leaving them helpless.

Evan Gilead came to stand at the feet of the motionless body, shadowed with a film of mud. He did not like Ed Duncan, did not bother to look at the man. He hated the handiwork, hated seeing another beaten and shamed. But John Stratmeyer had hired the brawler, swore he was invaluable. So Ed Duncan stayed. But that could not make the old man offer his respect or even his acknowledgment.

The old man brought his head up against the stiffness in his spine, straining to see beyond the body lying too still. A rare one this time, who had fought back. Evan felt the now-familiar guilt build in him, and the futility. He needed Stratmeyer to carry the ranch; he had no sons left to share the burden and the joy. He let his head drop back to his chest, watching the outlines of the motionless form.

Mary Gilead found her steps quickening, found herself cursing the long material that hampered her. It took only the smallest thing to defeat her. Where once she could ride herd with Evan and then come home to care for the babies, now she fought to step faster in the long woman's skirt that old age made her wear.

Something frightened her about the long form sprawled near the empty hay barn. A name caught in her throat. Joseph. As she came closer, the name escaped her lips. The length to the body, the pale brown hair too thick and tangled, the supple hands unlike his father's, so much like hers. The old woman winced as she saw one hand move convulsively in the mud and snow, fight to gather itself in a fist, then fail.

It couldn't be Joe.

They had been told by solemn prison officials that Joseph Andrew Gilead had been released a week early. That he had taken the money left for him by his father, had bought a horse, ridden away. That was two years ago. For long months she listened for the single horse, waited for the knock on the door. And Evan had waited with her.

After six months Evan gave up. He never spoke to her about his plans until one cold afternoon when a thin man with an unforgiving face and blunted manner came to the ranch, accompanied by a young woman who was his daughter. He would run the ranch, Evan said. He would cull the wild cattle, brand and ship the stock, and deal with the losses to rustlers. John Stratmeyer would live on the ranch, in the big empty house, work on shares, and become a partner in the Three V.

Evan no longer had the heart, or the will. She knew that. Their sons were dead or gone. Their daughters buried as small children. It was Joe's disappearance that had buried Evan's will.

Old Evan Gilead used his cane as a brake, leaning

18

into it to stop his forward motion and balance his crippled body. He could feel his wife come up beside him, could sense the touch before her hand came to rest on his arm. Stratmeyer and his daughter had gotten to the back barn before them, and John was kneeling in the churned mud beside the body.

The old man could see the darkened shape of blood soaking into the earth under the turned face. Mary's hand tightened on his arm, harder than he had felt in years, as John rolled the body over to lie on its back.

The head came last, twisting on the limp neck, coming with a jerk to settle back into the mud. Evan could feel the shock run through his wife, knew that it echoed in his own weakened frame. Her hands went to her face, to cover the widening, disbelieving mouth. Evan staggered slightly, jabbed his cane harder into the damp ground, and worked at the phlegm gathering in his throat. The words came out raspy and hard.

"John, wait. That's our son. That's Joseph Gilead."

Chapter 2

The old woman knelt slowly to the ground. Words went on above her head, confirming what she had known to be true. Her hand reached for the bloody face. Nine years ago this son had been a wild and laughing child, free with his temper, reaching to become a man. He had been a handsome boy, with thick light hair and large green eyes set wide apart in a soft-planed face. Eyes that mirrored every thought running through his quick mind. Taller than his father even then, with awkward arms and long legs not yet grown into their promise.

Now that handsome face was torn, flesh hanging from his forehead to expose the white bone. Blood pooled in a thickening crust at his nose, bubbling with each labored breath. She could see more white at the lacerated cheek, under a rapidly swelling eye.

This was her son, her only son, her baby child. Home from prison after nine years. Tears ran in split rivers down the lined cheeks, but there were no sobs, no sound. She had cried her last too many years ago.

Mary Gilead was not aware when others around her leaned down with strong hands to hold the bloody head. She did not care that her woolen clothing had risen above her laced shoes to expose the white fragility of her legs. This was her child, maimed, beaten, and finally come home.

Above the bent head of the old woman, men cursed softly and took their eyes away from the stilled body. Voices grew louder; one man moved from the gathering, heading for the corral and a fast horse. More noise, more booted legs moving erratically just at her eye level, hands waving in furious circles.

A face she recognized came to rest near her—Track Williams, long homely face, clear blue eyes, an old friend. He spoke something to her, and she nodded, willing to believe what Track told her. Then his kind face disappeared as if into a thicket of legs and bodies.

The thin face of John Stratmeyer hovered near her

son's head; she panicked and struggled to warn the man away. But as if in anticipation his face split into an obligatory, reassuring smile, then he lifted Joe's head, tilting the face until the blood no longer pooled down into his hair but found a new track along the bony jaw to soak deeper into the badly stained saddle coat.

They were taking him somewhere, lifting him carefully in preparation. The old woman felt panic sweep her again, until she recognized the serious faces of Track, the foreman, and a newer hand. Joe disappeared in their hands, and she was left alone in the mud.

Where was Evan? She needed him now, needed the strength he had given to her to hold their life together. She looked up. And more tears came to her, blinding her.

Her husband stood, balanced by the ever-present cane, stood and stared at the torn face and bloodied shirt, the fresh stains on the wool coat. There was nothing for him now; he had abdicated to John Stratmeyer.

It was a long struggle for Mary Gilead to rise. She wished for an arm to come down to her to offer help; she looked vainly for the Stratmeyer girl. Then she took a gulping breath and came erect. Her searching eyes found the girl hovering at the barn. Mary felt the keen cut of disappointment that the girl had not come to her. She turned to the house and to Evan.

Elissa could feel the old woman's regret. She gripped the corral post tighter. She saw the two old people, saw their need for each other, hands touching as they walked to the house. A brief and genuine smile covered her face at the sight, then died early, impaled on her thoughts of the unconscious man suspended between three staggering men, on their way to the security of the long ranch house.

She knew the story, heard the rumors. Her father was earning for himself what another man had thrown away in one horrible act. There were times when Elissa felt a vague guilt, standing at the corral, breathing the fine air of the secure valley ranch. This should have belonged to another. Now she knew who had lost what she had gained, had a face and a shape for him. She watched the procession, and the guilt was nudged aside by a blossoming hatred.

A soft nose pushed against her arm, a dark head peered at her, the whiskered lips twitching gently. She picked up the trailing reins and took hold of the blue gelding. She knew the doctor would be in soon, she had seen Des Harpwell ride out. There was nothing for her to do in the house. But she could put up the roan.

Her long fingers stroked the soft thickness of the winter coat, and she smiled at the balling of fur that came away with each touch. Spring shedding of winter's protection. The air was full of stirring hairs, thin lines of insects finding the renewed warmth of lifting currents. Anger came back full-force; white teeth caught at her lower lip. She straightened, pulling on the roan's bridle. She wanted to stay here forever.

Perhaps he would die from his beating. She knew Ed Duncan had fought for money and had killed more than once. He could have killed again. It was evil to think such thoughts; she knew that. But she did not want to move on, away from this ranch. Not ever.

The shallow noon sun caught the young woman's hair, lighting up the gold, drawing out the pale silver. The mother had given much to her child, as there was little but the height of her to come from the tall, dour man who was her father. Long yellow hair, strong brown eyes, a short nose dusted with freckles against pale skin that rarely colored. Her slender body was the more feminine, the curves more noticeable, for the whipcord length. A girl growing into a woman.

The voice steadied Joe, eased him back on the bed into the thickness of pillows. Then someone else tugged at his raised hands, pulled them away from the neck of the figure looming over him. He could see again, just barely. The red haze and spiraling blackness were gone, replaced by a blank throbbing in his head, a tearing across his cheek. The simple act of lying back down had brought fire to his back and side. He cursed in a low monotone, then stopped as his throat found its own pain.

Then slowly he opened his eyes again and looked up into the worn face so different and so familiar to him. His mother, aged beyond the nine-year span of time. Dark hair faded white, thinned to wisps, eyes vague, glassed with a myopic blue over hazel. The hands bothered him the most: reddened and lumpy, with all their grace gone, they lightly touched his cheek as if he would disappear under their pressure, washed him with a dampened cloth to wipe away more blood.

He turned his head from the hands, taking a long time to look around the room searching for the face he needed. The old man stood just beyond the seated woman, leaning heavily on a crooked length of wood. Joe gasped with the shock, and the answering physical pain was the renewal of his punishment.

The proud, strong man was gone. Old beyond the sixty-some years. Permanently bent with a visible pain, broad misshapen hands that held tightly to the round head of the stick. Joe couldn't look into the glazed eyes, couldn't bear to see the cloud that covered them. He twisted his head deeper into the soft feathers of the pillow, trying to run away again.

"Joseph, you keep still. Keep that head quiet, and I'll be done quick, so you can go back to visiting and sleeping."

Something else familiar, something finally comforting. The local doctor, a constant visitor during the days way behind him. A bit of sanity during the long time of the trial, the small cell, the dragging time. Joe steadied himself to look up into the round face of Edgar Travers. The man was almost ten years older and still had the cherubic look of a child. A slow smile threatened Joe's swollen face, a lopsided smile in answer to Travers's easy banter. A smile that disappeared quickly. Joe struggled to speak, and the words were thickened by his bruised throat.

"You still here? Good. I need a . . ." He found the effort beyond him and closed his eyes, to drift with the returning red haze that pushed into his head. Outside him he could hear the voices and the shifting sounds of the people around him. But he did not care.

"Mrs. Gilead, Evan, it's mostly surface damage, even the bruises on his neck. There'll be scarring, but he's fine. A few days of rest, some of your good cooking, and he'll be up and ready."

Then the doctor's voice dropped to where Joe could not hear. "What happens then I don't know. From the looks of him, prison was rough. We won't know for a while. We just won't know."

He didn't want to face the two old people somewhere on the other side of the bedroom door, but he couldn't stay cooped up much longer. He had managed three days inside the small room, and panic was pushing him.

When he closed the door softly in the early morning and walked into the once-familiar big room, he was aware of someone at the window, the one that overlooked the long distance to the Resolution valley. He turned to leave, reluctant to face anyone who lived in this house that had become a prison. Shadows hid the face of the person hunched in the old rocker, but he knew who it had to be.

"Glad you're finally up. Son." The word had to struggle past the drawn mouth. Joe stopped in his turn and came around to stand by the chair. It was another familiar place for him. Impulse brought him down on his heels to face the bent figure. He wanted to break the silence of the years, but stayed mute from the roil of feelings inside him. Minutes passed, then both men became aware that they had lost their chance, that others were stirring in the big house. Doors opened, voices murmured in sly talk. Joe stood.

"Thanks for the care. Sorry it all came to this. I only wanted to see if you and Ma were all right. I'll be gone today."

It was a struggle for him to stay by the chair. Muscles pulled against the recent bruising, banding in his breath and slowing him. But he was almost away before a hand found his wrist and took hold. Some of the old strength was still there.

"Son, it ain't going to be that easy. Your ma's been sent to her bed. Doc says it's her heart. You got to stay on now. For her, at least."

Chapter 3

Worry came easily to John Stratmeyer. As he held the shoulders of the unconscious man and felt the dead weight pull at him, worry knotted his stomach into sickening bands. Each time he glanced down at the still face, light brown hair falling from the bobbing head, swollen features inhuman, he saw only another move.

It was too much: another search for the next place, the next ranch that could be home for himself and his daughter. Stratmeyer looked up once, and beyond the two men struggling with the long legs of their burden, he saw his daughter with a strange horse, holding its bridle while she watched the procession. He would not be moved again.

Damn this Joe Gilead. Damn him for returning. John wasn't going to give up his rightful earned share of the Three V easily. He owned eighteen-months worth of shares now. They gave him a hold he would fight to keep. Be damned to the man.

It was the old man's bungling that had almost killed the Three V. Ed Duncan's presence had stilled the thievery for a while, then it had started up again. Small signs—a few missing steers, tracks of horses headed back into the badlands, a band of yearlings short counted—not great losses yet, but more than winter kill. Duncan stayed, and saddle bums skirted the ranch boundaries, but the problem was growing.

And John Stratmeyer was worried. He thought he had a solution, thought he could stop the rustling before it strangled them. And what he did not need was the interference of the prodigal son to slow him.

He felt the steep rise of the porch steps at his heel; he shifted the cumbersome burden in his arms and backed slowly, awkwardly shifting his high boots to find purchase on the narrow steps.

Stratmeyer turned away from the body once it was laid on the rope bed. He stopped to speak gravely to the Gileads, to offer his condolences, his apologies, his support. Then he left, grateful to be outside. A few words put the men back to work, and he was alone. With the needed time to think. His shadow made a concave line on the ground skipping ahead of him as he

27

crossed the yard and found the safety of the small pen. He stood alone in the welcome quiet.

"Pa, what's going to happen to us now? Where will we go; do we have to leave right now?" He jumped at the sound of the words; the questions echoed his own worries, and he had no answer. So he frowned at the impertinence of his daughter and shook his head, unwilling to admit that he did not know.

The next three days the ranch boss kept the men jumping at their chores, sorting out the feeder stock from early shippers, flushing out the ever-present strays, topping off the few broncs left unbroken. Finally the circuit wrangler came for his spring work, freeing another hand to ride fence and check water. They would need more working horses soon; the spring gather would start in another month, and John wanted everything under his control.

Twice now he had ridden to Hardin Fowler's Wagon Wheel, hoping to catch the rancher at home. There were questions that only Fowler could answer. Hardin Fowler had ridden with Hank Gilead for years, had been with him that last ride. It had been Fowler who'd fought with the drink-crazed younger brother, who had come awake a long time later to find his friend dead, his skull crushed. Hardin Fowler, rumored to have been wilder than the older Gilead boy, was now settled and married to a woman once sweet on Hank Gilead.

Hardin Fowler would have the answers, but Stratmeyer did not look forward to the visit. He didn't trust the too-friendly smile of the man, the easy gestures. But then, John Stratmeyer warmed slowly to any offer, any hint of a bond of friendship. The importance of the questions pushed Stratmeyer into making the ride one more time.

One booted foot found the stirrup of the stocky bay, and John settled in the saddle. Finally he would be talking with Hardin; a note sent yesterday had come back with a set time. He touched spur lightly to the red bay flanks and loped down the narrow track that would take him out of the Three V. He felt a fierce pride when he rode across these grounds. This was his home now, and he would fight for it.

Fowler's Wagon Wheel was close to the surprising cut of the Little Missouri badlands. It was poor land with thin soil, cattle were forced to wide range for basic sustenance. There were times when John wondered how Fowler made even his small yearly increase. The judgment shown in settling here only bore out John's opinion of the man.

Urgency made the ride shorter this third time. Stratmeyer tied the bay at a sagging rail in front of the small house and stayed a moment longer to ease the cinch on the horse. The animal's deep sigh was his reward, and he slapped the wet neck with a rare fondness. Shook was a good horse.

He took the rotted steps carefully. The front door opened, and a woman met him at the shallow veranda. Sunlight came through the badly woven roof in shattered lines, spilling a crazy pattern of light on her dress.

Her voice was soft and husky, pleasant to his ears.

"How do, Mr. Stratmeyer. It's a beautiful spring day. Hardin says to come right inside; he's in the office to the back. I'll bring in coffee, and something else, right away. You go ahead in."

John Stratmeyer nodded his greetings and stepped by the tired-looking woman into the house. Lucy Fowler stayed for a moment longer in the clean air. One hand went by long habit to tuck in a loosened strand of dull brown hair, and a smile flitted across her face at the rebellion of the escaping curl. The smile broke through sullen lines to expose what had been beauty. Company eased the loneliness, even ranch business company that demanded coffee and a bottle of whiskey.

She smiled again; Mr. Stratmeyer didn't look the type to join Hardin this early for anything more than a hot cup of reboiled coffee and quick words. He was a polite and contained man, a controlled man who gave only a rare evidence of his loneliness. It would take someone as isolated as she was to read the signs.

She turned to follow the visitor inside the house, smoothing her red hands over the worn rose printed dress. Company was rare out here, and she was going to take full advantage. As for Hardin, he would not dare curse her in front of John Stratmeyer and the power of the Three V. She smiled a very small smile at her own nerve.

The hearty words startled Stratmeyer: "John, good to see you. Come right in. Almost done here with Duke, and I'll be right with you." John snorted at the pre-sumptuousness of the man; he had all the right words of success and none of the strength to back them up. "Be right with you."

The soiled puncher barely glanced at the newcomer as Stratmeyer took a seat beyond the desk, ignoring the sullen-faced man. On his way out the puncher remembered his manners and nodded a short howdy, then was gone. Fowler stayed at his desk and waved a generous good morning to his guest, muttering something about pressing ranch business. John fought down his instinctive distrust of the man and rocked back in his own chair on the unbraced legs, feeling them give with the strain of his weight. He watched the younger man coldly.

Hardin Fowler was at ease behind the tilted desk; he pushed back in the arm chair and spun around to stare out the window, away from Stratmeyer's gaze. Past gossip said he had been a ladies' man, a real hell-raiser, and that Hank Gilead had ridden with him every step of the way.

Pushing forty now, the ruddy face was weathered and peeled to a deep burned red, and threaded veins laced his nose and cheeks. The stocky body was still hard, still capable, but with a beginning hint of softness. There was a thickening to his jaw, a red fleshiness to the expanse of neck bulging above the freshly ironed hand-made shirt. All signs to John Stratmeyer that the man was less than he thought. John shifted in his chair and got to business.

"Two reasons I come, Hardin. We got to deal with the rustling. I had it stopped for a while, but they started again. They took almost a hundred head this winter. The ranchers farther north ain't been hit yet, but you and me, we sit right on the badlands. We got to stop them before they bleed us dry.

"I thought to bait a trap and get me a trail to follow. I'm betting it will lead us right into the badlands. I've got twenty head of short yearlings that I'm going to put out below High Top, set a couple of good men to watching them. Grass is good enough to hold them three, maybe four days at the least. Be real easy pickings for them thieves. And we'll have our men right there to follow the trail.

"I'm here 'cause I got the cattle and one good man I can spare. But that one's all I can afford right now. Spring gather's got me short. I need one man from you, with enough supplies to last him those days. Figured you wouldn't mind helping out, seeing as they've been after you."

Stratmeyer finished his words and sat back. He watched as Fowler rubbed his nose vigorously, coughed twice, and then spat a stream of juice, hitting the tin bucket hard enough to make it ring.

"Why, surely I'll help you, John. Always ready to help the Three V. Got a few yearlings myself can add to the bait. And take Luff Engels, enough grub for a week. Can always bring it back down. That should do you well enough."

He couldn't miss the condescension in the words, the

tone of voice. Of course a two-bit spread like Wagon Wheel would be pleased to help the Three V. But the eager generosity, the flamboyant gesture of adding cattle, sending the ranch foreman, too much grub, irritated John's natural frugality.

The next question he hadn't put into words yet, so a silence settled in the small room. John coughed, uncertain how to begin. Then Hardin did it for him.

"Hear ole Joey Gilead finally made it back home. From the story going round, it wasn't too pretty a homecoming. That Duncan of yours can surely tear a man apart."

John was surprised at the admiration he heard in Fowler's words, admiration for Duncan's strength, acceptance and approval of the bloody beating, and no concern for his former friend. He nodded to the younger man, giving him his lead, willing him to continue. Hardin obliged him.

"You most probably want to know what happened them nine years back; bet that's your second reason for this here visit." His voice changed to a roar. "Lucy, where's that coffee at?" Then he continued. "If I was in your place, I'd want to know all I could about that there son. It ain't a pretty story."

Hardin did not look up or acknowledge his wife as she brought in a steaming pot, two cups, and a half-full bottle on a battered tray. John tucked his head in mute acknowledgment but kept his eyes on her husband. He took the coffee but barely bothered to refuse the proffered bottle. Hardin did not notice the tightened mouth of his guest as he poured almost a half cup of liquor into his coffee.

"Hank and me, we was friends a long time. Hank, he sure was a heller. All them Gileads were hellers, even the old man in his time. Hank and me run the ladies wild, drank everything we could find. Sure made his old man proddy, bailing us outta jail all those times. My pa wouldn't touch me, but old Evan, he always paid for me, same as his son.

"Towards the end, Joey started following us, riding just out of reach of Hank's temper, but always there. Could drink a sight more than Hank, and the gals went right for him, that baby face and those innocent cow eyes.

"Well, we hit over to Beach just after delivering a herd. Got to drinking and Joey got running a bay gelding he said was the fastest anywheres around. Some Montana waddy said he had a better jughead back at the ranch that would run the legs off that bay. We followed him out, took a bottle or two with us."

Fowler's face turned somber, his eyes almost gray, as he dug deeper into the memories. "That old bay surely went and lost to the Montana nag. On the ride back Joey found out that Hank bet the herd cash, bet it all, and lost. The kid couldn't take it, flew off that damned bay, and lit into his big brother. Broke a bottle over Hank's head, and it ended right there. Joe, he kept pounding at Hank and crying; I tried to stop him, but the son of a bitch downed me right pretty with a handy rock."

There was a long pause, as if Fowler were gathering his thoughts back from that bitter time. "When I came to, Hank was dead. Head smashed in and that damned big rock right nearby, all bloody. And Joey was gone, lit out running. Was near enough to morning that one of the hands came along soon enough, and we went for the law.

"It was Montana law that found Joe. Passed out, the other side of Beach. Covered with blood, shirt and hands filthy with the stuff. They sent him up to that new territorial prison for his seven years.

"Near to broke the Gileads. They got old plenty fast since Hank died and Joey was sent up. A real shame. Joey, he got only those seven years 'cause the judge said he didn't plan the murder, killed in a drunken rage. His own brother. Don't know where he's been the last two years, but it sure ain't good for you, and that pretty daughter you got, to have him coming back home right now."

John shook his head in disgust; this was more than he wanted to know. The waste of lives, the bitterness, and the pain. It was easy to see why Gilead had stayed to fight Duncan where most men would back down and run. He had nothing left that mattered. But Hank Gilead's death had given John Stratmeyer a chance, and he wasn't going to give up to the fair-haired son. He couldn't let the immediate pity sway him. He was going to fight for what was now his.

A curt nod and an end to the questions was John's sign that he was satisfied. Fowler stood ponderously, swaying slightly, and followed the tall rancher through the dark main room of the small house to the front door. He laid a big hand on the drawn shoulders of the older man, a gesture of sympathy and friendship that he knew was not wanted. The knowledge pleased him. Because Stratmeyer, despite his dislike, still had to come to the Wagon Wheel to ask a favor. Fowler grinned.

"I'll send Luff over today with the packhorse and supplies. He'll know what cattle to drive out to High Top. Good idea you had, John. Damned good idea. Should put us right on the thieving sons' miserable hides. You keep coming up with winners like this one and old Evan, he won't think of giving back your share of the ranch to his son. Good idea."

Hardin appreciated the distaste he saw rise in the other man's eyes. Good. He could hear the soft and tentative footsteps of his wife, the fair Lucy of the quiet voice and someday inheritance. He stood unblinking as Stratmeyer mounted the bay and left the small yard. The graze he so desperately needed for the future lay to the north, under the Rocking B of Lucy's distant father. She was the only child. So in time it would all be his, but he was beginning to tire of the wait.

Chapter 4

She had been very careful to stay away from the injured man as much as possible. Only once did Mr. Gilead ask her to care for him, to take in a meal and help. She did not look at the face while she lifted his head to spoon in the thin soup. But she could not avoid the wide green eyes that clouded with pain as he fought to sit up and move away from her touch.

He knew her thoughts, yet there was no demon behind the bright green light, only the vulnerable look of a wounded animal seeking shelter. Elissa remembered the shame she felt as those eyes met hers.

And the face—the thick pale hair that had once been short now grew ragged over his forehead and down his neck. Under the heavy fringe the green eyes looked through swollen flesh. A heavy planed face, the straight nose broken once, the mouth thin-lipped and bracketed with sullen lines.

She did not like the face, its brooding mouth, the unblinking stare, but she could see the old man in it, and even more of the old woman. The thought of Mrs. Gilead added to her distress. She could not bear to have the kindly woman bedridden. Visiting her was even more difficult, to sit beside the bed and touch the knotted fingers, the broad palm of those once-capable hands. Elissa loved this woman, was warmed by her generosity to a motherless girl. The gaunt figure tucked under the bright quilt made her hate the battered man who was her son even more.

Elissa leaned on the high corral railing. It was safer outside now that the son was up and moving about the main house. She no longer belonged in there, and she resented him the more for her feelings. But it was days like this one, the air warmed by a taste of the sun's heat, the sky clear for miles, little wind to whip up dust, that gave her peace for a few precious moments. She treasured these days.

The blue roan came cautiously to her, sniffing at the flowered elbow hooked over the rail. She eyed the tall horse, lean, high-withered, thinned down by miles of travel but with good lines showing, a depth to the chest, strong quarters, a clear eye. A good horse. She wished he would take his owner far away.

The voice close behind her made her jump, and Elissa added that resentment to a building anger as she turned to the intruder.

"That old son seems taken with you, miss."

Simple words, trying for some connection, making no demands. Elissa studied the face of the speaker and kept her silence, battling her flaring temper. The vivid bruises were faded purple; the torn flesh was healing slowly under the plaster strips. The face of Joe Gilead was emerging.

The years had to have changed him. The mother spoke of his handsomeness, and Elissa had heard the same from the few young women in Resolution. But the handsomeness was gone, lost to a sharp-edged suspicion. By the prison years she would guess. The once-pale hair had darkened to a dirty brown; the soft baby looks were angular and harsh, with old and faded scars crossed by the newer, deeper ones.

The eyes would be the same, shaded green, quick to read thoughts and see the hatred in the face before them. Elissa turned away from him, shame flushing her face.

But Joe had seen the look and could only wonder at the source of smothered hate. He had barely spoken to this child, had stayed away from her deliberately, guessing at the distress his return had caused.

He spoke to her back, resignation dulling the words.

"Miss, I'm no threat to you. I'm staying on for Ma. When she . . ." He stopped then, refusing the thought, and turned his head, searching for something. Then he spoke again, in almost a whisper, words that were meant to soothe.

"I'll be gone soon enough, miss. I have no claim left on this place. That died years ago. There's nothing for you to worry over on account of me, nothing that will change."

He put out a hand to the blue roan, and the horse stretched to the reassuring smell. Joe stroked the muzzle, cupping his hands to hold the soft lips. Then he patted the shiny neck once and walked away from the corral.

Elissa watched him across the yard, saw the stiff movement to his walk, the droop to his wide shoulders. Headed straight back to the safety of the house. Then something stopped the man, turned him toward the raw walls of the new equipment shed. She pulled at the length of her yellow braid; those words meant to ease her worry had done nothing but add fuel to a growing doubt.

John Stratmeyer reached over his head and found the heavy belt. It felt awkward buckled around his waist, riding high on his hip, the holster thong tight around his thigh. It made sense to wear a pistol now, with the renewal of the rustling, the spring gather, the winter slow snakes coming to the sun. And the man who stood outside, at the corral fence, talking to his daughter.

He saw her hands flutter in agitation, watched the man walk away from her, saw her tug at the braid. If she were younger, a child again, she would put the tip in her mouth and chew, or turn to him and run to his protection.

Her innocence choked him, blinded him for a moment. John shook his head and saw Gilead's long stride bring him directly opposite the shed door. No murderer was going to talk with his child; no killer had the right to speak to her.

Stratmeyer jerked the door wide and stepped outside. The man he wanted stopped suddenly, came around to face John.

"That's right, I want to talk to you. Gilead, you listen, and you listen real good." Damn the man, standing there polite as can be, showing none of the shame that was his, owning nothing but a quiet stare that heightened Stratmeyer's fury. He stepped out into the bright sun.

Joe saw the father's steps, saw his head turn to watch his daughter at the corral and then come back to him. It was easy to know what was coming, but the knowing why did not make the bile more pleasant to swallow. The man came too close to him, close enough for Joe to focus on the red face, the shining eyes full of righteous anger. This man owned a right to flay Joe, but Joe did not have to let the pain show. He was allowed some protection. He watched the man, let a heaviness come into his face, let nothing show as the words flowed over his head.

"Listen, you son of a bitch, you killer. Your own brother . . ." Spittle formed at the corners of Stratmeyer's mouth. "You've got no right to be talking to my girl. She'll listen 'cause of manners, but there's nothing you got worth saying to her. Nothing. She don't need to deal with the likes of you."

Joe jerked once at the damning words, then his face smoothed out, eyelids lowered for protection, wide mouth thinned to a line. He made the fingers of each hand unroll from a fist, made his arms hang at his sides. There would be no reaction from him.

"I can't run you off this ranch. Yet. But I'll make your life hell if you so much as go near her again. You hear me, killer?"

Stratmeyer could not accept the blank look, the easy slouch of the man. As if the words meant nothing, as if the epithets made no dent on the calloused mind of the ex-convict. Thoughts raced through him faster than their words would form. No man in jail had the right to speak with his girl; no man who'd murdered his kin had the right to live. Stratmeyer clenched his fists and felt the nails dig into his hardened palms. And the anger rode him beyond common sense.

Joe almost stepped back, almost brought up his forearm to defend himself from the fist that targeted his mouth and split tender flesh against hard teeth. His head spun around, and he stepped back to balance, but his hands stayed to his sides. And the brilliant green eyes stayed on the man's face.

John Stratmeyer stopped himself before striking out again. The bastard, the monstrous gall of the man. Staring at him, blood leaking from his lip, face blanched white. Not moving, not answering the challenge. Giving him nothing to fight. John Stratmeyer knew his hand rested on the slick butt of the pistol, and he pulled the weighted gun from the leather, letting its heft keep the long barrel pointed down.

Even this threat did not move the man, did not erase the bright green stare or move the long body. Nothing crossed the hated face but the network of scars. There was no stopping now.

The gun barrel came up, and its glistening surface shattered the sunlight as it cracked against hard bone. Drops of blood slid from the oiled metal as John's arm followed the power of the swing. A woman screamed; a horse whinnied. And Joe Gilead dropped to the packed earth, butt first, elbows coming to instinctive rescue as the long body slid in the dirt, skidding from the unleashed force.

This was right. This was what needed to be done. To have the son of a bitch laid out on the ground. This was where the killer belonged. At the feet of good men who did their jobs and protected their families.

John Stratmeyer wiped the oiled blood on his pants and resheathed the pistol. Then he walked over the triangled legs and headed toward the house. He had work to do.

He stopped once, five feet past Joe, and did not look back when he spoke. "You're warned. You stay away from my daughter."

The pain was a relief, a focal point to draw him away from the almost-empty big house and the two shadows that lived there. Joe did not feel the blood's warmth as it soaked his collar and ran down along his neck. The pain was right and clean, given to him as a reminder. He had almost forgotten, had almost given in to the sweet memories and tired faces that offered love and forgiveness.

He pushed to his knees and rested, then came to his feet in ragged movement. There was no one in the yard, only a bright noontime sun that shafted into his eyes. Joe turned by habit to the old barn and raised his head only after a few steps.

The girl was there, by the high railing. Her hand was raised to her mouth, her eyes cloudy. She almost took a step toward him, but Joe shook his head, and she stopped.

He had to close his eyes then, and when he opened them, she was gone, and he was completely alone.

Chapter 5

Evan Gilead watched the doctor gently put the pale hand back on the bright yellow quilt. The man stood ever so slowly, as if unwilling to risk any quick movement that would disturb his patient. Edgar Travers came out of the darkened room just behind the old man; they walked together down the stairs to the comfort of the small room to the abrupt left, the room where all ranch business had been carried out for years.

Travers sat down heavily and waited for his friend to settle. He found it hard to begin.

"Evan, I can't lie. She is going to die, and soon. Very soon. Her heart is weaker every day, and sometime in the next weeks it will stop. I am truly sorry."

Evan had to turn his head sideways to see the round and bland face of the young doctor. A good friend despite the age difference, a friend for the past ten years. And now this. He spoke almost as an afterthought.

"Joe will stay until the end; he's promised that much. But I tell you, Edgar, I don't understand nothing about the boy. He says nothing, does nothing but sit with his mother, and leave when I come to the room. I want to make peace with the boy, but he turns away from me. Hank's dead, and Mary's dying. He and I got to live out what's ahead. I don't know."

The thin voice trailed off, the thoughts unfinished, unspoken. Edgar Travers could add nothing that would take from the old man's sorrow. All that was left was to sit and wait.

"Damn." John Stratmeyer stood at the gate and cursed the day. All his men were out, mending fence, checking stock, riding the canyons for strays. Harpwell was on his way to High Top with Luff Engels and the herd. And down here one more man was needed, right now. "Damn."

He squatted and ran a practiced hand down the bay gelding's leg. Heat, tenderness, an unwillingness to put the hoof down square. Track Williams had seen it this morning, had told the boss his best stock horse was looking gimpy on that off fore. John swore again.

He had made his plans with the horse as part of the day's chores. That big roan stud had to be cut, a job really for two men, a job John figured he could handle alone with the bay horse as help. He could depend on Shook to keep the line taut and hold the hammerheaded roan down. Long enough for John to do the job.

The roan had come in with the four-year-olds earlier in the spring. Bad luck for all of them the roan had finally been caught. Still entire at seven years, the strawberry-colored horse was a menace. Stratmeyer would just as soon shoot the son, but the old man was firm. Cut him, break him, and use him. But no shooting the big horse.

It made no sense to John: the roan was poor quality stock, good for nothing, and not worth the men and injuries it would take to break him. But the old man wouldn't let this one go; the roan was to be cut and then ridden.

John stayed for a time longer on his heels, hand stroking the hard black leg, wanting not to feel the heat just above the tough hoof. The bay put his nose down to touch John's hair, whuffled through wide nostrils as if to ask what was happening. Stratmeyer cuffed the black muzzle away, but gently, unwilling to admit even to himself that the bay was special.

A goddamned stone bruise. He could even see the blood mark deep in the flaking sole of the hoof. Nothing but a deep stone bruise, but to use the horse would risk further damage. Time would heal the bruise, toughen the now-tender sole, but that time left John in trouble.

A heavy pink head came over the railing, thick forelock almost covering the small eyes. John rose from his heels and shook a fist at the pig-eyed horse. The roan accepted the challenge and half reared, squealing in anger at his solitary confinement. The half-broke stock had been herded to the larger pen, leaving the stallion alone.

And leaving John alone to face him. Even the wrangler was gone, on a small and clever paint, to ride with Track Williams to Wet Springs camp. His daughter was in the small town after a cut of cloth and extra flour. The strawberry roan snorted once, a long fluttering sound from deep in his chest.

To hell with it. He saddled a nervous chestnut and coiled a good rope to the horn, then thought better of it and went to the ranch store for another rope. One would not be enough for this battle. The chestnut would do, but John could feel a slight trembling to the horse, an edge of fear that would make it unreliable. To hell with all this, he'd rope out that damned son and finish the

46

job, then get to his other work. He swung up on the shifting horse, then urged it forward with quick jabs from his spurs. The chestnut was reluctant to walk closer to the big horse behind the high lashed fence.

Then the chestnut stopped hard, jolting its rider as he was concentrating on coiling the second rope. John looked up to find Joe Gilead facing him, seated on the tall blue gelding, loops of rope held easily in one hand. The circling stallion stood to watch, ears flickering from the sweat-darkened chestnut to the tall gelding, quiet and alert under the soft touch of his rider.

"You need an extra hand for that one. That strawberry'll be tough."

John couldn't believe it: Gilead's words were noncommittal, offered to allow John his pride. The man's hat rode cocked on the brown hair, letting air get to the half-healed welt above his ear. The welt Stratmeyer's gun had put there. Was there nothing the man's pride could not take.

The first impulse was to shove the offer aside, but common sense and a second glance at the red-eyed head over the top rail dampened the hatred. Stratmeyer nodded his acceptance, then tossed a coil at the blunt challenging head. Both men watched the big animal plunge backward from the attack, whirl to the far side of the corral and stop with head high. A long whistling defiance came from the thick throat, a challenge that let the riders open the gate and ride inside, set themselves with a wary eye on their opponent.

John's right hand held the rope; Joe kneed the blue

to move the stallion. The chestnut shied as the rope went on to settle on the thick crest of the pale strawberry roan. The horse went up high, waving his forelegs, squalling a threat to the men and horses below him.

Then the big horse came down running backward from confining rope. The chestnut kept an uneven pull on the rope, then at a signal from his rider took two steps forward and halted again. The unexpected touch of freedom staggered the roan, sent him down and over in a wild roll.

Another rope snaked out to set a small loop over the flailing hind legs; the lanky blue horse went backward in quick steps and drew the slack tight, hanging the heavy roan between the two sturdy horses.

Stratmeyer watched the ease and grace of the tall rider and his speckled blue gelding. He could not deny the quick envy that came with the sure throw and ready response of the blue. Then the two men faced each other over the strung-out body of the struggling roan.

As boss it was for John to dismount and work on the exposed scrotum of the tightly held victim. He slipped his feet from the stirrups and tensed himself to dismount. The chestnut threw its head in nervous response. Gilead spoke quietly.

"The blue might be better at holding by himself; want me to cut? I've done it before."

When he thought about it all later, he would marvel at the simple words that left John his authority yet had him follow each suggestion. And a tiny bit of appreciation would crowd into his mind, to hover there for future reference.

John looked at the scarred face and the green eyes, searching for the signs of contempt. He saw nothing but a man sitting a good horse, waiting for an answer to a question. John looked over at the trembling roan, sweat lathered on the pale coat, turning it to mud in the corral dust.

"Yeah. That blue's a better horse. I've got the knife. Here." He flipped the carefully honed blade at Joe with an easy underhanded throw. Joe caught it handle first and came off the roan in one swing. The man took time to pat the wet flank of the frantic stallion, then made two cuts with the sharp blade. The horse screamed shrilly.

The high-pitched wail echoed against the corral railings, and the chestnut reacted to the skull-searing sound, leaping sideways away from the newly gelded stud. Tension on the rope loosened; the heavy headed roan found the edge of freedom, and the horse fought to raise its front end. Joe was caught by the ponderous body, flung around by the wildly pawing front legs.

John spurred the chestnut hard to the right and laid the reins into the horse's neck, demanding the animal step sideways and back to hold the line. The horse threw its head and leaned for a long instant into the spur, panic destroying the years of schooling. That one instant longer gave the strawberry another chance.

Joe felt the flank of the roan slam into him, knew a moment's fear as the knife slipped from his hand. He grabbed instinctively for the blade as he rolled beyond the struggling horse. Blood coursed over him from the two widening gashes between the roan's hind legs.

He found the blade, felt it cross his palm; there was an instant wetness in his left hand, a burn that turned numb. He fought to keep away from the massive neck and shoulders of the rising horse. He yelled at the blue, hying the horse back with slashing moves of his right hand.

The blue steadied himself from the contagious panic and took the two steps back, then another two steps, straining into the bulk of the downed horse, pulling the sitting animal's hind legs to one side, sending the horse over in an unbalanced heap. Stratmeyer's chestnut answered the spur-driven cues and backed away from the thrashing gelding. The two horses laid the bellowing roan back on the corral floor.

The dust settled slowly, the chestnut let out a great gust of air, and John Stratmeyer found himself finally breathing again. The lanky blue stood braced at the end of the rope, holding the hind legs still. The chestnut horse shook between John's legs but held steady on the choking line to the thick neck.

Joe Gilead sat halfway between the bleeding meat that was the new-cut gelding, and the obedient blue. He made no move to stand but held the wrist of his left hand with his right, watching the steady drip of bright red from his palm to mix with the torn ground and the darker blood from the gaping wounds between the great horse's hind legs.

The green eyes came up to meet with Stratmeyer's hard brown ones. The boss took his time in assessing the damage—a cut hand, shirt torn across the right side most probably from a flint-hard hoof, a too-strong flow of blood coming from the subdued roan. Joe Gilead said nothing. He sat in the dirt and waited for something from Stratmeyer.

The stillness went on too long. John found nothing in himself that would save his pride while acknowledging the increased debt. Without Gilead he would have been pulverized between the strength of the bulky roan and the treachery of the chestnut. He owed a debt to the silent man he did not want to pay.

The thin sound of material tearing brought two sets of ears up, and John shifted uncomfortably in the saddle. He watched the man wrap the torn piece of cloth around the bleeding hand and then come stiffly to his feet. The voice carried far in the stilled corral.

"That donnybrook opened them cuts too much, need to stop the bleeding or you'll lose him. Got some wound powder and a heavy salve?"

The matter-of-fact treatment released John. He told Joe where the medicine was and held the chestnut still while the man came back and finished doctoring the defeated strawberry roan.

The ropes were loosened from the downed horse and coiled to hang back on the horns. The gelding still lay on his side, wide-sprung ribs heaving in great gasps. The fight had gone completely from the animal along with the masculinity. Flies collected in the exposed slashes, stuck in the thick salve covering cut flesh, and the horse barely flicked an ear at the added discomfort.

John had to reach down and spank the wet flank of the big horse to stir the animal into rising. Head down, ears tilted, the roan swayed on trembling legs to the corner of the corral, unmindful of the two horses in what had been its territory less than one hour earlier. The gelding was complete.

John slapped the chestnut's shoulder. "Stupid of me to think I could trust this bronc. I would have been better off on foot." The words were more than inadequate. He knew the silent rider had saved him from a savaging, yet he still could not find the thank you.

He had to say something. He nodded at the blue horse. "Damned fine horse. Could do with more like him on the ranch." This was not enough, and he knew it. Shame flushed his face as he swung the chestnut around to hide the heat. The two men went from the corral in silence, one man on a sidestepping chestnut, the other walking slowly, leading a quiet blue.

Joe stopped. He spoke without looking up at Stratmeyer. "I don't want to go to the house with this." He held up his wrapped fist. "Need clean bandages and a shirt. Don't want to scare anyone in the house. I'll be in the small barn."

John finally looked down at the man angled beside him. The shirttail wrapped around his hand was soaked red, the fist tightly clenched. Here was something he could deal with, a way he could help.

"I'll send someone down with salve and bandages,

some hot water. You put up the blue, and it'll be right along."

Joe walked the blue to the back barn, glad to be away from the uncertain temper of the foreman. He was almost out of hearing when the words finally came. "Thanks for saving my hide, Gilead. Owe you one."

The throbbing in his hand kept him occupied. Even this hurt was better than the pain that came with the image of the dying woman in the big house. Her pleasure was to take his hand and wrap her fingers in its calloused grip. It was like holding a fluttering bird; the hand jumped and twitched inside his. His fist tightened with the thought, and a new pain made him look down.

Blood came in thin lines from between the fingers, soaking the bandage beyond saturation. Joe peeled the soggy cloth away to expose the slash. Dirt mingled with the blood, and sand was embedded in the flesh. He went to the outside of the barn and pumped a shallow bucket of water. Its clearness turned a rosy pink with diluted blood as he left the hand in the numbing coldness until the flesh tingled.

There was nothing left to do now but wait. It had taken him time to learn the skill, but prison time was a strong teacher. Back inside the old barn he settled on his heels, leaned back to the old planked wall, closed his eyes, and went still inside.

No one inside the house, no one moving about but his daughter. John pulled at his chin. He would need medicine and water, a clean shirt, a rolled bandage. His daughter could not tend the man. He would not allow her.

"Papa, I saw what happened out there. And I know what needs doing. You cannot deny him this."

Her arms were loaded with piled bundles; her eyes flashed a warning. John opened his mouth. "He . . . I . . . that cursed roan." She pushed by him. "He is a man, and he saved you. He is their son, and we must do this for them." John Stratmeyer had no more words to stop his child as she left him in the sunny kitchen.

Fear kept her moving, fear and an unnamed relief. The big door to the barn was open; the late sun was angled to outline the man. Sitting motionless against the wall. Elissa stopped. It was as if someone were painting her a picture. Of Joe Gilead and his prison.

Light layered across him in thin lines through shrunken boards. One hand hung loosely from his knee, fingers splayed wide. The other hand was loose-fisted, resting palm-up on his left knee. She could see red beading along the exposed wound.

His head rested on the wall, eyes shut tight, neck and throat arced and vulnerable, shoulders slumped from the corded neck. Then the eyes opened slowly, and the head dropped as if too heavy. And the man leaned forward, put out his uninjured hand to push away from the wall; he was at an angle from her, and she could see the paleness of his skin through the torn shirt. A deep sigh escaped her as she stepped through the doorway.

He turned from the sound and faced the girl. She

stopped suddenly: there was too much of the old woman in those eyes. In silence she held out the bandages and the can of ointment, the fresh shirt meant to cover his vulnerability.

The alarm wired through him faded as Joe knew who stood at the door. He took what she offered.

"Miss, thank you."

It was awkward dressing the wound, difficult shrugging out of the torn shirt. And the girl did not move, did nothing more to help. The softness of the old shirt went on easily over new bruises. It was one of Hank's shirts, with darning high on the right sleeve, near the shoulder. From a tear when Hank had fled a mustang he'd roped. Memory clouded Joe and brought a tightness back to his face.

The girl moved away from him; fear brought her hand to her yellow braid. Joe shook his head.

"Miss, I don't mean to scare you. Please, you and your pa both. Believe me, I won't be staying to take a thing from you. The old man wants it that way; I want it that way. I'll be leaving soon enough."

Then this man who frightened her so, angered her, backed away and turned to the wall. She watched the long body shudder once, then straightened as he came back to her. The voice was soft, lacking its former bitterness.

"I'm no threat, ma'am. Tell your pa. Just let me be for now. Thanks for the help."

She did not move, nor did she offer any help. She stayed and watched the man work over the lumpy dressing and then go to a stall where the blue was tied. She had been dismissed without further thought.

But still she did not leave. A flooding of thoughts confused her. The kindness of the old woman was in the man, and the toughness of the old man. There was a special glint in the eyes that overwhelmed her with anger and something more disturbing.

When he spoke these same words to her before, she had scorned them. But to hear them spoken again, to watch his face closely as he made the promise to leave his home to strangers, drove the words deeply into her mind, and forced her to begin to believe.

Chapter 6

His pa always told him he'd come to no good. Trying to rope the cow instead of milking her. Wrestling the calves to the ground and coming up all covered in manure. Man was meant to work with the Kansas land, not ride hell for breakfast over it. That's why Des Harpwell was in the Dakotas. It was a land that liked a good horse and a long rope.

But right now Des Harpwell figured his pa maybe was right. The old slicker didn't offer much warmth against the bitter wind and rain that had come at them for over a day now. Damned lucky there weren't snow mixed in just for the pleasure.

And Luff Engels weren't much on company. The swelled-head son just sat under that damned scrub tree and only muttered short reply when Des tried some friendly-like conversation. This baby-sitting a herd a no count cows wasn't what he came to the wild and woolly west to do. No, sir.

But Des had to admit the boss's plan made some sense. Stuck up here on the high bluff, they could take turns checking over the rim, watching the small herd below chomping on that sparse graze. But they couldn't be seen from the Little Missouri badlands, and it figured sure to Nelly's bustle that that was where them rustlers came from and rode back to. If you knew where you was going, the sudden ridges and twisted canyons were passable, but an uneducated rider would be lost inside forever. And Des, well, he knew his limits.

The squat puncher took his time wriggling up to the lip of the mesa. His turn to wallow in the deepening mud, to lean over without his hat and check on the herd. Des put his hat to one side, very carefully; earlier he'd been in a hurry and put the durned thing down upside to. Almighty wet inside there when he finally got to putting it back on.

His yellow hair, plastered to the round skull, made his pitcher ears more pronounced, gave his nose plenty of space to lead the parade. Des always allowed he sure was no beauty. But he could dance and knew how to smile at the ladies. A few more days of this nonsense, and he'd be back to visiting one gal in particular.

There was someone behind him; he could feel the shape of him. Des spoke in low tones, wary of the sound carrying, even in the driving rain.

"Luff, can't see nothing. Boss did say to wait three,

maybe four, days. That's to meaning we can split this soggy dog town tomorrow if we still got them critters."

He didn't expect an answer from the surly bastard; they'd sure had this conversation before. Des just liked to hear something besides the thin rain and the rustle of his own clothing. Luff dug him sharply in the side, harder than need be, even in bunkhouse horseplay. Des rolled back to look at his companion and voice his complaint. He only got to turn his head, and the sharpness became a hot and spreading pain that stopped his breathing and widened his eyes.

He made the effort to finish that roll and looked up at a familiar face. Not Luff Engels, but a man he knew, a man he'd seen at the Three V, the ranny who beat up all them drifters. He put his hand to the burning inside him, felt the handle of a knife at his ribs, coughed once. A rush of blood flooded his mouth, drowning him in its warm thickness.

Des struggled to lift his head, looking for Luff. He had to be somewhere. All he could find in the darkening rain was a stilled form up at the stunted tree, wound in the torn slicker with the odd red patch. He knew he'd found Luff.

Another cough brought him almost to sitting, then the fiery pain pushed him back to the new comfort of the wet ground. He watched as Ed Duncan walked to the bluff edge and waved his arm in a quick salute to someone below.

The last thing Des Harpwell heard was the reluctant bellowing of a scrubby herd of beef being moved off their graze before they were finished.

"Duncan, that was a specific order, to check with Harpwell at High Top and come back. You land here two days later smelling of a still and with nothing to report. Mister, you're fired. Pick up your gear, and I'll have your pay ready. You get yourself out of here in a Texas hurry."

John Stratmeyer thought he'd seen it all in his fifty years. But Duncan took the words and the firing with a smile and retreated meekly to pick up his gear. The man'd lost a good berth at a big ranch, and the son was smiling!

He could only shake his head and go on to the growing problem. Duncan had nothing to say about Harpwell and the Wagon Wheel man. It had been four days since he'd sent them out. Still short good hands, John faced having to make the trip himself. He snorted in disgust.

And then he saw the Gilead son come from the big house, stop to lean on a post. Even at this distance, John could feel the quick eyes scan the yard and breeze past him. He could feel the instant rise of short hairs at the back of his neck. Anger clogged his throat and choked him.

They had not met since the gelding of the roan. The horse was a skeleton now, infection draining the big frame of its ugly vitality. Turned out with the young stock, the horse moved slowly or not at all, followed by a cloud of flies. John tried doctoring the animal, but there was little hope for the roan now.

Stratmeyer stretched to ease the pinching at his neck and wondered if Gilead felt the antagonism that engulfed him. Then he relaxed; here was an extra man. One hand went up in curt summons to the man across the yard. John half expected the command to be ignored yet wasn't surprised when the tall man came down the steps and walked slowly toward him. Gilead had been a cowman once. New anger flooded him with the almost-charitable thought about the man. And then Joe Gilead stood in front of him, face hidden by the sun, head turned away from John. Damn the man.

"Mister, you know this land better'n most. I need someone to ride out to High Top and check out the bait herd. Got to be real cautious. I don't want to spook the thieves if they haven't gotten to the cattle yet. You could make a start now and be back midday tomorrow. Tell Cookie I sent you for a day's rations. And make it fast."

He half expected a protest or refusal. The command had come heavy-handed, wrapped in obvious dislike. There was no need for the man to take the order. John stiffened as the wide-spaced eyes came around to meet his for an instant. It was rare for the man to look straight at anyone, but when he did, the message was clear. Back off; leave it.

Stratmeyer kept his ground. He was pushing, but the men on High Top were his, and he was worried. A flash of something harsh came across the angular face, then Gilead spoke and the ordinary words blanked out the clarity of the past minutes. John Stratmeyer sighed unconscious relief.

"I'll need a rifle; got a handgun wrapped in my roll. Won't need a ranch horse; I'll take the blue."

That was all; that was his acceptance. The man walked wide around John, headed to the closeness of the back barn and his gear. Stratmeyer was left with a building anger, and a sense of a decency in the man that battled the facts. To hell with all the thinking; the job was going to get done. He knew that much about the Gilead son and his given word.

Joe eased the saddle on the roan, smoothing the patched blanket first. In the corner of the old barn, still hanging on a wooden peg from one stirrup, was an old saddle, a gift on his sixteenth birthday from a proud father. That was the day he'd ridden the cream stud. Pa had been proud to bursting from that ride, even though Joe had finished with a snapped rib and a beaut of a bloody nose.

The roan shifted its weight and huffed against the pull of the wide cinch. Joe eased the pressure some, aware that he'd been taking his anger out on the horse. A few more quick moves and the horse was bridled, the canvas roll tied behind the high cantle. He still had to stop at the cookhouse for grub, but that would take only a minute.

He was eager for this ride; he knew High Top and the land beyond it well. It held a wild beauty that drew a man. As a child, much younger than his teenage

61

brother, he'd been gone for hours in the maze of the river land, safe on a pensioned-off buckskin. He knew the land better than most, almost as well as the ancients who had hunted and lived within the confines.

The faint echo of the three-beat sound startled Joe. The old man was making his crab-stepping away to the back barn where Joe was trapped. He swung up on the blue and pushed him through the wide open door. They passed the old man in a long trot that became a run before the last line of corrals. Joe could not face the bent figure, the face canted sideways to look up at him, the thickened hands that shook as they gripped the rough walking stick.

Father and son had met once since that early morning. They sat together on heavy chairs in the big room, and the old man asked his questions in a low and hesitant voice. Questions about the prison years; careful questions about the faded scars that were laid across his hands and face, and wrapped in purple welts across his ribs.

The answers had been brief and blunt. Joe sat before his father wrestling with the need in the still-strong voice, to accept the love that came from reaching hands and clouded eyes. But he kept his face averted. He listened to the questions and gave factual answers that did not satisfy. It was the only time Joe allowed the old man to corral him.

Two hours of letting the roan run on and then come back to an easy jog brought Joe to the edge of the mesa, the last barrier between the soft swell of the range land

and the jagged edges of the river basin. He stopped to let the roan blow. It was coming dark and would be black by the time he reached the trail to High Top. His mouth quirked into a short smile: he had no grub; it would be a cold camp and a long night.

A circling of buzzards was visible as he rode closer to the bluff. Something had died up there. The birds were scattering now, but they would be back in the morning.

The predawn light took its time. Wrapped in only the damp saddle blanket, Joe sat out the night huddled deep into the high bluff wall. The roan grazed companionably on a short picket rope.

Once saddled and bitted, the horse stamped restlessly, eager for a long drink of water that the morning air promised. A short sip offered from Joe's hat had not been enough for the high country horse. Joe mounted and set the blue to the steep trail climbing to High Top. He leaned his weight forward to ease the effort. Above the stiff creak of his saddle, and an occasional grunt from the laboring horse, Joe could hear only his belly roll with hunger.

Cresting the top, Joe sat the huffing blue and let him blow out, waiting with the certain knowledge of disaster pressed inside. The circling shadows were again plundering the thin camp up ahead. In the bright spring sun they had landed and were feasting. Joe spat out a bitter taste and put spur to the roan.

Rocks thrown at the great birds finally drove them away, ponderous in flight, bellies swollen with food. Joe screamed at the ugly birds. He had no worry about the rustlers hearing; whoever had left these bodies behind would have already taken the cattle. Men and beast were long gone.

The smell came first; the sweet putrefaction of decaying meat. Once dead, man become nothing more than useless, spoiled meat. Joe prodded the torn bodies with the toe of his boot, then bent down to look more closely. He averted his eyes; these were no longer men. No longer Des Harpwell who had been one of the few at the ranch to remember him, to offer unjudged recognition. He hadn't known the Wagon Wheel man, but the body was just as dead as Des, smelled just as badly.

Vague muddied holes were left by the bodies. Rain washed the prints of one man, a big man using the rain as cover. He'd used a knife, quiet, efficient, driven between the ribs directly to the lungs. An expert in death. The poor bastards had choked on their own blood and died soundless and alone. Harpwell lay on his back, and if the birds had not gotten to him first, his eyes would have been open to the fresh blue of the endless Dakota sky.

Shaming weakness flooded Joe, loosened his knees and brought him retching to the ground. When the gagging left him empty, when the sweat on his face and body had dried, he stood up and turned away. There was much to consider.

Burial would be on the high bluff, and burial on the wild mesa, closer to the sky than anywhere else, seemed a good place. The digging took Joe a long time, and he made no distinction in two graves. He went deep enough for two and rolled the men in together, wrapped in drying saddlecloths. They had died together; let them rest together.

He did not know them well enough to impose on them his shattered beliefs. Harpwell had been a simple man from the Kansas plains. It took Joe a moment to find the words from his childhood, and he spoke them in a hesitating, stumbling voice over the new mound of sand and rock. Quiet words about "Yea though I walk through the valley of the shadow of death, I shall fear no evil, for thou . . ."

When it came his turn, when it was time to bury him, there would be nothing said over his grave. He would be buried far from here, buried without ceremony or honor. But these two men, murdered doing their job, would want something said over their last bit of earth.

He turned away. The blue roan nickered softly. Joe worked quickly, piling a mound of gear and clothing where he had found the Wagon Wheel man. He even retrieved the trampled hat from the rim edge. Someone would come back for these useless things if they were important. Otherwise they would become a bitter headstone.

Joe took the roan down the steep side of the bluff into the edge of the badlands. The roan watered in great gulps at the lip of the Little Missouri. The only tracks his rider saw were of a small band of wild horses, and the ever-present split prints of small deer. There were no signs of driven cattle or ridden horses.

He sat the quiet roan for a long time past the watering,

staring out at the violent land. Badlands. Named for man's fear of them. But holding their own beauty and life that could draw a man in to his own slow death. Something was out there now, hiding in the convoluted land, that was strangling his father, destroying the life he had fought to build from the endless land.

It was the thrashing of a small rabbit that shook Joe back into the day. He touched the roan and swung the horse away from the swollen river, back toward the ranch, carrying inside himself the awfulness of his news.

Chapter 7

Joe snugged the eager blue and did not acknowledge the tossing head and sidestepping jig. The blue snorted, trembled, tugged against the unexpected pull on the curb. Joe did not respond.

He rode head down, eyes vague, drawing no comfort from the good grasslands they traveled. Finding no interest in the wandering tracks of a single wild horse that crossed their path repeatedly. The tracks were fresh, the scattered dribbles of manure less than an hour old. The blue found slack in the reins and stepped into a trot. Joe felt the change, and his legs wrapped by instinct around the barrel; his hand found contact with the wet mouth, but he had only a corner of his mind on the eager blue.

There were dead men riding with him, and an old man unable to walk, an old woman dying. Their weight slumped his shoulders and dulled the edges of his instincts.

The blue roan spooked violently at a dip in the trail, nostrils wide to pull in a strange scent, ears pricked forward almost to touch, head high against tightened rein. Joe could feel the big heart pumping furiously between his legs. The horse's erratic behavior finally forced him to look up and see what was before him.

A dead mustang on its side, a mare from the looks of the small bundle lying between its hind legs. And a figure bent over the form, rubbing along the small back, trying to help a newborn foal to rise. A bay mare stood tied to a low bush, tail swishing indolently against early flies, uninterested in the activity behind her.

As Joe steadied the trembling blue, Elissa Stratmeyer looked up from her urgent rubbing and stopped absolutely still for a short heartbeat moment. Then she busied herself with the frail babe and spoke to Joe without bothering to look back at him. Her words were unmistakable.

"Help me. The mare just died, and I can't get the foal to stand. I need your help; I can milk out the mare and bring the foal back to the ranch, but I need your help."

It came to Joe slowly to ignore the pleas and ride on. One look at the dead mare and the unresponsive foal, and he knew the efforts were misplaced. The mare had been too young to be bred and give birth, and the foal was that sickly cream of many of the worst scrubs, a foal not worth saving. But he took an extra moment to look at the young woman, to search her face raised to his in silence. There was a bright shine of tears in her eyes, despair plain on her high-colored face.

Still he sat on the blue and watched as the young woman turned from him to work over the foal, finally raising it without his help. Its front legs were crooked, the knees offset, the tendons drawn up, so that the youngster stood knuckled over on the soft front of its hooves. Joe could only shake his head at the folly. The foal tried to nicker and staggered against the girl.

He tried, but the words would not come out right, the tone was harsh, roughened by a mounded grave on High Top. "Leave it, miss. Leave the cursed thing to die. Don't do no good trying to save this one. Look at those legs."

But the brown eyes, bright with anger, tears wiped away on a dirty sleeve, came up to stare at him, to demand that he do her bidding. Elissa spoke rapidly, her temper flaring at the man's utter indifference to the pitiful foal.

"You get down from that damned perfect horse and help me, mister. And do it now."

Her father was in the voice, but the face and figure were of a woman grown. Against his own judgment, Joe slid from the off side of the blue and knelt with the girl to add a steadying pair of hands to the foal's wobbling balance. The heads of the man and woman almost touched across the narrow damp back, and Joe inhaled the warmth and female scent. A woman's scent, a woman just past being a girl. Like the young

68

girls he had chased so many years ago. But there was nothing here for him.

Elissa looked straight into him as if she could sense the rise of feeling in him. Her bitter, knowing gaze made him drop away, brought a haze of memory to dull his mind. But she wasn't going to let go.

"I know the foal's nothing. I can see those legs, those tendons. But even the worst sinner deserves a chance. You should know that. And I seem to be the only chance this baby has. So you keep her steady, and I'll milk out the mare. The body's still warm."

She put her hand to Joe's arm to rise, and she could feel the muscle jump under her weight. He looked at her too quickly, shifting his gaze when she met the green eyes. Her own words went over in her mind, in an endless repetition, her own thoughtless words spoken in anger to the kneeling man: "Even the worst sinner deserves a chance." No wonder he would not look at her.

She went to the restless blue and took the canteen from the horn and emptied the water as she walked to the pale corpse. Joe could hear her grunt as she lifted the stiffening hind leg of the dead mare and rested it on her shoulder. He could hear the steady short streams of milk being forced from the drying bag. Those first gulps of milk meant life for any new being, and the young woman was making certain her orphan had that much chance.

The bay mare accepted the foal slung over her saddle with little fuss. Joe gave his hand and bent knee to

Elissa, and she scrambled to the broad back of the mare, just behind the cantle, where she could ride with both hands on the rocking foal.

The rest was up to Joe. He mounted the blue and picked up the bay mare's reins. It was a continual battle to force the blue to a slow walk, to urge the bay to move out with her double burden. The mare would not be hurried, and the odd procession made a cautious march back to the long valley and the Three V. It took two hours and more for them to walk the less than seven miles.

Chapter 8

"Found both men dead. I buried them there, up on High Top. No sign left, nothing to read. No cattle, and no tracks; the rain took everything."

That was it. Two men dead. John Stratmeyer sat back in the old chair and watched the scarred face of the speaker, wanting desperately to blame the man for the deaths, wanting to strike out at the hateful face and watch it disintegrate under the force of his blows. But his long frame stayed relaxed in the leather-backed chair, behind the desk, secure from his own temper.

The moment passed. Joe Gilead showed no signs that he understood the silence. Stratmeyer's anger grew as he went over the few words again, heedless of the man shifting against a growing restlessness. There had to be something more.

"What do they want; why would they kill for such

70

scrub cattle? How did they even know Des and Engels were up there? Someone had to tell them. Damn it, Des Harpwell was a good man."

Speaking the words made the loss real. Stratmeyer's fist slammed the desk twice, sending papers to the floor. Then John remembered and looked to the impassive man standing before him. The familiar rush of hatred came back.

There was a lot he owed the man now, and John hated him the more for the debt. There had been no mention to the old man of the pistol whipping, and now Gilead brought in John's daughter and her misplaced project. And had buried a man for him on High Top.

The words came no easier this time. Joe Gilead was a threat, and there was nothing John would say.

"You can go. It's done."

Something pushed him to rope out a fresh horse and slap his old dusty saddle on the high withered back. He buried his head in the safe motions of snugging the cinch. He did not want to look at the old house or stay in the quiet of the back barn. He did not want to know the old woman lying in the house, dying.

Death behind him on High Top, death holding the big house, death riding beside him with the face of his brother. Joe dropped the heavy stirrup, and the slapped leather spooked the horse, made Joe grab for the bit shank and talk quietly until the animal stood steady.

He lined the horse toward town. He had been a long time returning to Resolution. The sorrel's easy jog, the bright sun, new buds on low bushes, greened tops of winter brown grass—he gave in to the warm sensations. Anything to keep his mind from endless circling thoughts.

Stillman's store and saloon hadn't changed. One horse tied to the front railing, a buggy mare backed up to the loading door. Joe looped the sorrel's reins and took no note of the other horse, of the silver-studded saddle and fine-plated bridle, paid no attention to the elaborate brand on the near quarters.

Stillman's was the same; a new barkeep with an old face poured the acid liquor into a waiting glass. Joe's two bits disappeared into the apron pocket, and the barkeep went back to the high stool and his soured reading.

There was another man in the room, shadowed at the corner table. It didn't matter to Joe; he didn't ride here for company. The amber liquid burned a raw fire into his belly, washing the sight of two newly dead men. He coughed and banged the glass hard. The barkeep appeared, this time leaving the bottle when he saw the weight of the coin. Joe raised the glass, lost in the liquor's deadening relief.

"Well, if it ain't the little brother. Something must be pushing at you to get you in town. Resolution ain't too fond of you, Joey. But me, hell, it's right good to see you, kid."

The voice was an echo; the hand reaching for the bottle in front of him was unsteady, freckled, dirty. Hardin Fowler.

"Thanks for the drink, kid. I'll share it for old times'

sake, for the good memories. There was some good time, Joey. Some wild times, just you, me, and Hank. We done some riding and some howling back then."

The voice rubbed the edges of his control. Words not said, meanings left open. Joe caught the wide wrist as Fowler went for a refill and threw the arm away from the bottle, spinning the man with the effort, turning on his own boot heel to finally face the speaker.

"Well, goddamn. Look at the kid, will you. All growed up and feisty. Thought that would of been whipped out of you by now. Good to see you, Joey. Been a long time; nine years if I remember right."

Hardin kept talking, wanting to do anything to stand Joe Gilead back from him and find a quick exit to the horse outside. Goddamn was right. The pretty-boy kid was gone, replaced by a man alone and unafraid. It took work to keep his eyes to the face before him, but Hardin knew the rules and knew he was lost if he gave way. This weren't no drifting puncher, no prison-whipped dog; this was a man who'd seen it all and didn't give a damn. The wet-eared kid had sure disappeared.

"Son of a bitch, boy. You sure scared me grabbing my arm that way. Just wanting to share a drink with you, remember the good times we had. You know I married Lucy some time after all the fussing was done. She was mighty sick there, but she made me a good wife, a good woman. I know she meant a lot to Hank."

Remind him, back him off, keep him pinned by the words. Talk enough, and that anger'll go from the eyes. Then he could get out of the saloon in one piece without losing ground. Hell of a time for the kid to come home.

"Now, Joey, you know I never done you no harm. Felt real bad about that night, as if I was to blame, not holding on to you better. But you was a wild one that night; I couldn't . . ."

Fowler babbled on, and the wave of words broke the control in Joe's head. His hand went to the gun strapped at his thigh, and something flickered past his head, out of sight. The worn grip of the gun felt right in his hand, then a click behind his right ear stopped his arm in midswing, and the gun barrel stayed pointed down, resting on his leg.

Joe came back enough to see fear consume Hardin, then relief wipe out the stain. Fowler grinned at him, and a door slammed behind him, and footsteps came alongside him. Day and time came back as a voice spoke at his ear. "Joe, put the gun away. That's no good." The voice was familiar, reassuring. The doctor, Edgar Travers, his one friend in Resolution.

"Stillman's man came to get me, said there was trouble brewing. Put the gun back, Joe. I've come from the ranch. Your ma's doing better, been calling for you."

By turning his head Joe could see the wide-muzzle shotgun inches away, the grim face of the barkeep at the far end of the stock. The man let the barrel drop but kept the twin hammers cocked. Joe heard Fowler's loud release of breath and found himself taking a big gulp of air. The gun slid easily back into the holster.

Fowler opened his mouth to speak and shut it as Joe's eyes came to him. Behind Joe the doc held up his hand

and shook his head. For once Hardin kept silent, backing up two steps and muttering to himself. He missed the dislike in the doc's face and did not see Joe leave the bar. In the short time it took him to find his table, the unfinished bottle from the bar in his hand, the big room was emptied, except for the expressionless barkeep high on his stool.

Travers waited at the sorrel's shoulder. "Joe, it wasn't smart for you to come in here. Towns like this never forget, or forgive. To the law you've paid your due, but to these folks you're still a killer.

"I'm sorry, Joe, but it's the truth."

He waited, letting the words sink in, giving the man time to hear the rest. "Your mother seems to be reviving some. I'd get back there if I were you, soon as possible. Seeing you will be good for her. Give her a reason to come back."

Joe moved as if the words meant nothing. He mounted the restless sorrel and swung from the doctor and the hate-filled town of Resolution. His right hand stayed to the swell of the saddle, and he felt his fingers tremble against the hard leather, knew the echo of anger deep in his belly. The hand slipped to his thigh, fingers digging hard into the long muscles. He did not look back at the puzzled Edgar Travers.

God, he'd wanted to kill Fowler for his talking. Raging fury still burned in him, the same flame that had killed Hank. Joe dropped his head, loosened the grip on his leg, and felt a wetness in his eyes. It would never go away.

75

He rode the sorrel hard from Resolution and did not see the tired speckled horse pulled to a stop at the side of the road or the lank-haired woman sitting on the wooden seat, mouth open to call, one hand raised as if in greeting. He flogged the sorrel and raced toward the wide ranch lands.

She was so still in the marriage bed. The long body was barely visible under the heavy layering of quilts, most of them made by her hands over the years. Joe went in quietly and sat in the stiff chair. Her hand had turned over to lie naked and palm up, supplicating against the yellow star pattern that was her favorite. Age had spotted the white skin, wrinkled and twisted the long fingers. Something burned in his throat as he touched the knotted hand, lightly stroked the creased palm.

Her eyelids fluttered, then opened, at his touch, and Mary Gilead saw her son, head bent against his thoughts, one hand curled around hers. She wanted to tell the boy it was all right, that everything was fine, but she could not remember why such words were important for him.

She only knew she loved this son, that he was special to her, so much like his father in temper and spirit. She struggled with wandering images: Will sprawled at the bottom of the canyon wall, smelling of whiskey even in death; Henry lying beside him in the small cemetery. Henry, willful, wild, spoiled. But it was this one, this youngest child, who had survived, whose bowed head was near to her yet beyond her touch. This one had the fire and the depth that kept him with her, even through the nine years absence. So like his father, so special to her.

She fought her fight, knew that there were words of importance that she must give to this son. "Joe." Her voice was a hoarse whisper that brought the scarred face close to her, near her mouth. She wished for the strength to finish her words. "Joe, we love you, your pa and me. You're a good man, Joe, please. . . ."

The old voice faded; a rustle of sound came from the tilted head and neck, a sound made familiar to Joe in the seven years of hell. Then the long sigh came; he could almost mark its passage from between the sudden red of the wrinkled mouth. The relaxing of the fingers' tentative hold on his hand was the final sign. He sat for a moment longer with the body, letting a force that burned in his chest rise to his throat, scald his eyes. He waited. But the relief was not there for him.

"Stratmeyer, you bastard. Get out here." Joe stood in the empty center of the ranch yard, yelling to the man he knew worked in the small office.

"You think you're going to get this ranch from me, figure you can run it your way. Hell, you couldn't run an anthill. You left two good men up on High Top. Ask them about your orders. By god, you need your ass kicked from here back to that damnable mesa. Get out here, goddamn it." The last words rose to a screaming pitch.

And they stayed hot in his throat, the bitter sounds

ringing in the quiet of the afternoon. A few heads poked from the bunkhouse, and one man came up from the corral, diverted from his chore, dragging a half-coiled rope. Doors slammed inside the house, and footsteps hurried across bare floors. Joe could hear the three-beat sound of his father, the slam of the wide door, then silence. He looked up to the darkness of the long veranda.

The old man had stopped at the top step. Behind him stood John Stratmeyer; coming along the veranda on either side were cowhands, the cook, the wrangler. Joe was alone, facing the angry line of men.

Strong hands picking him up when he'd fallen, the coolness of the deep veranda in the summer heat, the big tree hugging the sluggish stream, the corrals and their endless churning livestock—all were gone now for him, driven away by one drunken night. All that remained was the dead body of his mother, alone in the shade-darkened room.

"What's got to you, boy?" The question came from Stratmeyer; the words sounded like his father. Joe picked up his tirade.

"You ass-licking bastard, moving in where you don't belong. This was mine till you came . . ." He could go on, the words boiling inside him, pushing him, but a slashing motion from the heavy cane in his father's hand silenced him. He'd said enough.

The effort was painful to watch, but the old man straightened his back, lifted his head to look at the tall young man in the middle of the yard, legs apart, eyes colored brilliant with fury. This man was a stranger Evan had thought was his son. Hatred flamed in the strong face; fury rode the wire-tight body. This was a man he did not know.

"Boy, you were staying for your mother. Well, just maybe you best leave now. She won't really know you're gone. You said enough."

The rest of the words he must speak were a greater pain to the old man than the pull of aching tendons and shattered bone.

"I hoped you weren't like your brothers, hoped there was something of your ma in you. But you sound like Hank on a drunk. Get out, boy, and don't come back. This ranch don't hold nothing for you now."

Joe had what he wanted. A gift that rubbed him open and raw. He walked away from the old man and the foreman and missed the glitter of satisfaction in the man's lean face: He ignored the bewildered faces of the hands, the shock pulling Track Williams's grin out of place. He shoved aside the memory of the inert body deep inside the house. He had stayed long enough and had gotten what he needed.

Elissa was barely aware of the noise outside, the shouting, the heat of tempers, as the struggling foal kept her kneeling in the deeply bedded stall. The baby was trying to stand on her own, knees buckling, bent legs crossing, and Elissa feared for the small body, worried about it slamming into the hard walls. She looked up only when she knew someone else was in her barn, someone who brought horses inside her haven.

Two horses. The lanky blue roan, still sweated and tired from the High Top ride, and a blocky bay gelding with a crooked blaze. She stood abruptly. Her father's horse, his special mount. And it was Joe Gilead slapping his old hull on the solid back, Joe Gilead slipping the bit into a dry and resisting mouth. The bay knew only her father and threw his head violently at the touch of strange hands. She heard the hard curses.

She came out of the stall then and stood in the path of the bay. The roan was haltered and long-roped to the saddle, a bedroll and two canteens were packed to the bay, and Gilead was struggling into the heavy coat. He did not see the young woman emerge from the stall, and jerked hard on the bit when the bay shied at her presence.

The harsh words spun him around. "You can't take Shook. That's my father's horse. You'll be nothing but a horse thief. My father would never let you ride that horse, you or anyone else."

The words were an accusation and a truth that pricked Joe. But this was what he wanted. "Miss, out of the way. I'm riding out now and taking this horse with me. It's a poor trade for the ranch."

He looked straight at her this time, not turning his head or dropping his eyes to shield his thoughts. Shock stopped her next words. She had never seen this Joe Gilead.

She had grown to think of the Gilead son as emotionless, drawn cold by the prison years. But the man who looked back at her now was alive, eyes emerald in fury, face ghost-pale with thin lines of the uncovered scars. Now she could believe that murder was in him, even the murder of his own brother.

Fear stopped her, and she watched him mount the restive bay and dig unforgiving spurs into the sturdy sides. Horse and rider burst through the partially opened door, with the reluctant blue following close. Elissa ran with him and saw the bay reach a gallop, scattering several men who had come from the bunkhouse and pens.

She went to her father and watched his face as he realized which horse Gilead rode. Only the tightening of the deep lines at his mouth let her know the anger. He turned to the bent old man beside him, spoke low murmured words meant only for those ears, and shook his head in disagreement at something said in return. Elissa glanced at the growing number of silent men as they watched the disappearing dust of the two horses and wondered what had happened.

Chapter 9

Before he knew the name, Ed Duncan recognized Joe Gilead. He knew the look, the set to the mouth, the restless checking of the eyes. A graduate of a prison, somewhere, sometime. Not Duncan's school, but the mark was indelible. He'd shaken his head in grim approval when he learned the name; that Montana prison was hard-time.

All things came around to Ed Duncan. Stratmeyer's

pinched face was no surprise; Ed knew he'd be fired for the nonride to High Top and had a ready smile for the man, a grin for the bitter words of firing. He no longer needed the Three V; he had another source of information waiting for him.

It had been no surprise when Hardin Fowler had beckoned him to the back of Stillman's big room. It figured that Fowler would finally recognize in Ed the signs of a dishonest man; Fowler himself carried a real easy set of signals.

And Duncan had read those signs early on. A restless man running to whiskey fat, a man dissatisfied with his land, contemptuous of his wife and her family, without the guts to make a move big enough to grab what he wanted. Fowler often sat in the big, almost-empty room in Resolution, pouring drinks "all 'round," complaining about poor graze, the miserable bastard he had for a father-in-law. All the good grass the man claimed the other side of Medora, and running only a few head on it. To Duncan's mind, Hardin Fowler was a man with many dreams and little ambition. Easy pickings.

The job with Stratmeyer at the Three V had been a fluke, a bit of extra money doing what he enjoyed. He'd been siphoning off good stock from the area for over six months when the foreman offered him the work, right in the heart of the good pickings. A bonus that gave Duncan a good laugh.

The big foreman was so bound by a narrow mind he never suspected the slow-moving bully, never thought the man could do anything beyond taking orders. A strict conscience would never let Stratmeyer comprehend the beauty of signing on to work for the very ranch that supplied the stolen cattle, the ready cash whenever Duncan felt the need. The thefts had slowed down for a while, but now he'd call in more men and make one big last raid sometime this spring. The Resolution valley was no longer of much interest to him.

Duncan's cellmate for two years had ridden the Little Missouri badlands and talked forever about the small hidden canyon that would support men and cattle, well beyond the reach of the law or the ranchers. Just before his release, the man had fallen to his death, and Duncan held on to the secret, storing it for the future.

Finding the canyon took him four blundering weeks; finding the men to ride with him was easy. The names varied, the type never did; men wanted somewhere for something, men too lazy to work for their thirty dollars a month and found, men with slippery eyes that no decent rancher would hire. Duncan was their leader without question; his strength convinced them as soon as they hit camp.

He finished the last of his drink, belched in approval of the burning liquor, and signaled for a refill. Hanging around this barnlike room for the past days had brought him a pair of aces and a stray queen in news. He grinned to himself.

Joe Gilead had shown new colors. Called out Stratmeyer, called the man a son of a bitch, stole his own damned horse. The law was interested in Gilead now, such law as there was around here. And Stratmeyer had yet to deal with the two dead men on High Top. Local respect for the man slipped each day the deaths went untouched. The Three V was losing power, coming closer and closer to Ed Duncan's reach.

The last piece he didn't know how to use, yet. The old woman was dead; Mrs. Evan Gilead was being buried today up on the bluff overlooking the Three V valley. The doc figured it was the fussing over the theft of the horse, the loud yelling from the ranch yard, that had finished her. Duncan hadn't got it yet, but he knew there was something here that would belong to him. An edge he could use.

The twist of irony did not escape him. Desperate about the two dead men, John Stratmeyer had ridden to Fowler's Wagon Wheel, talked about the deaths, apologized to Fowler for his foreman. The fool, spouting off to Hardin, asking his suggestions.

It had been Hardin Fowler who'd given the plan to Duncan, Hardin Fowler who'd told him where the men were camped, why they were there. Fowler had only wanted to warn, but Duncan had a better idea. And Duncan owned the man now, bought him with two dead men.

The big man stretched his arms over his head, reaching high and grunting with the strain. Then he brought his hands down hard on the bar and turned the few heads toward him in the noontime glaze of light. The room was emptier than usual; the old lady's dying had drawn spectators. But Duncan wasn't going to join the curious: he was headed across the border to a small

Montana settlement without a name, to start the word on the invisible telegraph that he needed men.

He pushed open the half door and let it swing with a vengeance. As he stepped off the walk, checked the cinch on the powerful gray, and poked his foot into the stirrup, Ed Duncan wondered if Joe Gilead planned on attending the proceedings. The law would be expecting him.

From a cut in the high bluff, Joe watched the gathering become larger as the time neared. From his stand across the narrow valley, he could even see the individual faces, watch the expression change from social talk to sober sympathy as the men and women paid their respects to his father. John Stratmeyer stood just back of the old man, hands clasped behind his back, dark suit and high crowned hat enhancing his thinness.

It was the girl who surprised him. Grief showed strong on her pale face, drawing the life from it in tears and shadows. He had not expected honest grieving from her. Edgar Travers stood near, one hand ready for support as the young woman swayed sideways in her pain.

Damn the man. The words blurted through Joe. His thoughts could not get beyond the curse, could not deal with the jealousy that rose in him as he saw the doctor's healing hand touch the girl's elbow. He raged at himself; there was no room now for such feelings.

He could not watch his father. Still sharp in his mind was the clear picture of the old body twisting violently to bring up the seamed face and faded eyes as Joe raced the stolen bay through the yard. He kept seeing the misshapen body, the glint to the clouded eyes.

The eyeglass Joe had to bring the services closer to him had once belonged to his mother, handed down to her from her father. Joe had found it packed with old shirts and a heavy long coat, some letters and a small metal locket with a braid of hair. He had taken the glass without asking but left the musty contents in the battered trunk.

Now the glass let him share in the slow ceremony taking place apart from him. He could see the preacher mouth the words, bow his head, raise his hands in supplication. Then the fresh wooden box, long and narrow, with a small flower carved in the center of the nailed top, was carefully lowered into the fresh-turned ground. The ease of the six men in handling their burden was evidence of the lightness of the body within.

Joe closed his eyes; behind the lids was the stilled image of the preacher, mouth wide, distorted, speaking endlessly the rote words of every death, every burying. Joe had spoken these same words over the mutilated corpses left up on High Top. But those bodies could not be like this fresh body; they were torn, pulled apart, bleeding from the wound made by their betrayer, from the necessary opening tears of the great birds that would return them to the earth.

A battle began to replace the peaceful memory of the frail body lying under the clean yellow of the star quilt, to make that picture into a companion of the massacre he had discovered. A cry came from Joe Gilead, his eyes flew open and he blinked against the brightness of the sun, the red lined vision of his mother.

He picked up the glass to watch again. The grave was mounded over, and now the mother lay next to her children. Joe could almost hear the sound of the first dirt clod shoveled onto the coffin. He had stood there in chains for Hank's burial, and that memory joined with the scene before him. Even the law was there this time, as the last time. The county sheriff from Bismarck, the local deputy, the new governor. The old man pulled a lot of weight in his grieving.

Enough. Joe slipped from the crumbling rim and forced his way back through clinging brush to the tethered bay. It took no time to retie the roan, check the cinch, and mount the bay. The familiar simplicity of the motions settled him. He pushed the horses up the end of the narrow split, cautious of the crumbling sides of runneled earth. At the top he urged the bay over the lip to the flat land. He would ride on without looking back, would not hesitate in his next moves. But he found the bay reined in to an unwilling stop.

It could not be helped. He raised himself above the old saddle and put his hand on the cantle, turning his head and shoulders with the effort. Directly across from his two horses was the gathering, milling around the new and old graves. The rawness of the new dirt was a shocking yellow in the dull soil. People were moving slowly, splitting apart in small groups to walk deliberately, heads bowed, to their waiting buggies that would take them to the ranch house just below the rim.

Unwilling instinct pulled his eyes to the slow-moving old man and the young woman who waited for him, restricting her steps to match his. The sight of her turned him restless again, and before he settled back to the saddle, the bay hit a high trot across the soft land, pulling the reluctant roan behind him. Joe let the bay run, urging the horse to more speed when he showed signs of slowing.

The bay was guided in a specific direction even in the erratic gallop. What was ahead was Joe's gift to his father, his final gesture of repentance. The loud words with Stratmeyer, the deliberate theft of the bay, his absence at the funeral—these were signs Joe laid out for the thieves.

He would find them, find the small canyon that held them, and offer a greater knowledge of the badlands, of the unknown trails leading to the backsides of wide valleys, box canyons rarely used. This was his trade for their acceptance. And then he would know the leader, would set a trap and clean out the predators.

He urged the bay, slapping the white lathered neck with the split end of the reins, fleeing the last few steps of the old man as he reached the black-fringed buggy. The solitary vehicle left on the windblown rim.

Chapter 10

Lucy Fowler watched the old man during the funeral services and the young woman who stood beside him so protectively. Nine years past it had been Lucy standing between husband and wife as they mourned Hank. Now she was to one side, alone, her husband off with his big plans, and she felt only a great pity for the old man, and for herself.

The pity turned to a bite of jealousy as the daughter put her hand on the arm, seeking balance from the heavy cane. Lucy had once hoped to be the daughter, to be the son's wife and bear the grandchildren.

Now there would be nothing left for the old man, no continuation of his line. His wife's blanket-wrapped body was covered by the drying earth, and the only remaining son was running from the law, riding a stolen horse.

And she was married to Hardin Fowler, Hank's closest friend, rival for her attention from the time she turned fourteen and the two young men discovered her blossoming figure.

It had taken too long for dreams to die. At the end, she knew the weakness in both men, and her own lack of strength. Hank died knowing she carried his child; she faced his death knowing he had not wanted her and the child.

After the sudden death and prolonged trial, Lucy had lost the small seed growing in her, had sickened and almost died. The town of Resolution believed her sickness came from grief. They would never know the truth, that she had been used and scorned by Hank, had sickened from her own despair.

Hardin knew the truth. And still taunted her with it, playing with her when she showed signs of rebellion.

He had stayed by her bedside, talked with her father, used her sickness to join them. There was nothing for her but to marry Hardin once she could stand. Her father told her it was good common sense, that there would never be a better offer.

Lucy Fowler walked to the old gray gelding, standing hipshot between the shafts of the battered spring wagon Hardin left for her use. Hardin had the big sorrel, saddled with a fancy Denver rig, a silver-worked bit in the horse's mouth. She drove with patched reins and a wire-repaired collar that rubbed the gray-speckled coat raw.

Lucy stopped. She was too close to the old man in his slow walk to the buggy. Shyness held her back from talking to him, so she looked back at the two graves, the raw new one and the sunken lines of the older one. Hank's grave. She could never forgive his abandonment, but the memory of his touch, the feel of his hands, still caused her to stir restlessly. Hardin never moved her in that way: he only took her harshly and moved his weight from her, leaving her in the dark.

She raised her head against the heat of the sun and looked out over the long valley and the high butte beyond. Dust focused her indifferent gaze on a pair of horses, a single rider, stopped momentarily on the far side. One man, leading a haltered horse, riding a stocky mount.

The face was indistinct, but the long body and easy grace as the rider twisted in the saddle caught at her. So like Hank, so like the coltish Joey only a few years younger than she. The rider had to be Joey. She was glad he had come to the funeral.

She thought to raise her hand and salute, but the rider twisted back to settle in the saddle and put the horses into a run. Lucy hoped the old man had seen. It would please him to know his only son had not forgotten.

The drive back to the small ranch she now called home would take a long time. The gray was old, pensioned off too late as a stock horse, lamed finally from bowed tendons. Good enough to get her around was what Hardin told her when she complained. Mindful of the horse, Lucy found herself bound to the house, forever trying to sweep clean the wide-spaced floors or pin curtains that would cover cracks around the loose-hung windows.

The gray moved slowly, his driver slumped over in the hard wagon seat, hands folded lightly around the lumpy reins. Once every so often, Lucy thought to flip the leather across the white back, chirping an encouragement. There was nothing she could contribute to the gathering at the Three V, no fresh-baked cookies or steaming pies, no soft, consoling words. She was too ashamed to say her sympathy to the old man.

Little came through her thoughts as she lurched with the motion of the wagon. The sudden halt of the gray threw her forward, and she put out a hand to stop her fall. Something sharp pierced her palm, and she swore out loud, shocked at the sudden sound and the use of the forbidden words. Lucy Fowler had been brought up properly.

"Damn it." She thought she heard laughter and looked up to find Joe Gilead sitting a chunky bay, hands cross on the horn, a blue roan snugged to the rigging by his knee. She felt color rise at the quick laugh, and then she let the years disappear.

Joey Gilead. A wild one around his brother and Hardin, but with a kindness, a special gentleness that let him ride out early to watch the sun, made him look up in wonder at the ragged flight of geese. She had never accepted his killing of his brother. The memory brought back the doubt she'd drowned throughout all the intervening years. She eyed the intruder. This Joe Gilead could frighten her.

"Joey, leave me alone. You're nothing but trouble, and I'm late. Hardin will be worried. You let go of that bridle."

She didn't miss the smile that covered the grim face at her words. This man knew Hardin too well. Then she caught her lip and blew out a quick breath. It was the same Joe Gilead she'd seen in town. One look at the face and she saw the years written on it. But the gentleness was still there, hidden deeper now, but still there. She knew that.

He spoke, and his words settled her back in the seat, made her regret her quick-tempered anger from a minute past. There was no meanness to this man.

"Lucy, you're still beautiful."

Then the voice lost its softness, became flat and hard. The new Joe Gilead could frighten her. "The old man, how's he doing? I saw you at the graveside. Near him.

Lucy . . ." The harsh voice fell away.

"He cried, Joe. I saw the tears. He loved her so. He even took the time to look at me and smile. I always envied you your family. He smiled at me.

"She died alone, that's what he kept saying, over and over. I heard him, saw him cry. To die alone, that seemed to hurt him the most."

Joe's hand came up, his eyes turned a muddied gray. "I was with her when she died, Lucy. Holding her hand. She forgave me. She was dying, and she thought to forgive me for killing her son. I have no right to that forgiveness."

"He's not alone, Joe. I watched the Stratmeyer girl. She's with him now, caring for him. And he reached for her hand, walked with her. He's still got someone. Not like you or me." The rise of self-pity stopped her words.

And Joe wanted to deny her words. She had a husband, a ranch. But he knew Hardin Fowler, and so he looked at the once-pretty girl he had adored, who was now a worn and faded prairie wife, old beyond her years.

Lucy picked up the reins and winced as the large sliver went deeper into her flesh. Joe saw her grimace, and old feelings came through his guard. He slipped from the bay, wrapping the reins around the whipstock. Wordless, he sat beside her on the plank seat and reached for her hand. Using the tip of his knife, he gently worked the blade around the long slice of wood. Then with his teeth, he pulled the inch-long splinter from her work-hardened hand.

For a brief moment Lucy felt all the old yearnings for Hank build up inside her. The long body was so close, the top of the head bent to her, over her hand. She closed her eyes against the memory. Then Joe's head came up from her hand, and he wiped at his mouth, smearing the droplet of blood that had come with the splinter. He closed her fist gently, holding her by the wrist.

Close enough to feel the rawness of the scars on his face, close enough that the older scars showed through, Lucy stared into the once-innocent eyes. They had narrowed from the years, the elements, the intrusion of others. The once-handsome face, ruined by the physical marring of battles lost and won, still held a glimpse of the past they shared, the good times of laughter and unknowing youth.

She leaned forward and placed her mouth against the thin-drawn lips. She held him to her for a long moment. She could feel his warm breath come in and out of her mouth, could taste the saltiness of his skin. There was a past sweetness to the contact that tempted her, then she opened to green eyes that she hoped were hazel. Sad green eyes that held a suspicious brightness.

"Lucy, believe in me. Don't listen to what is being said. I'm going to fix things for the old man. I have to. Please believe in me."

She watched as Joe slipped from the wobbly wagon to the back of the bay and jerked up the head of the tall blue roan. One hand came around in partial salute, then he reined the horses in front of her, across the track and

94

down toward the Little Missouri badlands.

She picked up the reins carefully and took mental note of the small bead of blood in the palm of her hand. It would heal soon enough, scab over and be gone, just like the reawakened memories would disappear.

She shook her head and cursed the gray. The gelding did not appear to notice. Off to the right, the dust settled slowly, as the horses and rider slipped into a swale just out of her sight.

Chapter 11

Instinct and old memory brought Joe to the canyon trail. The tired bay placed his feet carefully on the sudden downhill path. Over the past days Joe had learned a hard respect for the blocky animal. He rode high and easy over the saddle, giving with the jar of the quick-strided trot as the horse picked his way.

The wildness of the basin was as he remembered. Harsh and jagged rock split away from leaning walls and lay heaped in violent formations across the brittle ground. The exposed colors ran in convoluted lines, following waves of time. Unexpected trees and brush clung to the slanted pitch of the walls; spindly stalks of wildflowers, sparse grasses, tried to cover the exposed earth. Life here came from the ever-winding flow of the river, its slow and wide course giving way to deep, rushing spillways driven between narrow rock.

This time of year the river was wild and dangerous. Joe kept the two horses to high ground, careful to water only at shallow inlet pools, avoiding the pull of the white-topped waters. He knew the horses were tired, could feel their slow steps echo in his bones. Yet he was driven to find that one canyon.

It was easy to swing with the bay's strides, easy to go blank with his thoughts. The smashed skull rode with him, so badly broken that the undertaker nailed the coffin shut because there was nothing left for the family to see, to grieve over and touch. That was all he knew for certain. He had no memory of the fight, of the death of his brother. He knew only what he'd seen in the open coffin. Hank dead, Hank's blood on his shirt, Hank's murder held in his own hands.

Nothing had taken that memory from him, and the past weeks added to the burden. Sitting with the old woman, watching her struggle and die. Joe shook his head against the engulfing pain; he lost his sense of time and rode the bay by habit, moving against the horse's motion.

The echoing boom of a rifle brought his head up, made him haul on the bay so that the gelding sat down and then half reared, the roan jamming into the wide bay rump. The trail had gone into a familiar gorge, and Joe knew with a quick certainty that around the bend was an unexpected widening valley, a valley big enough to hold men and horses.

He sat immobile on the trembling bay, steadying the horse with a soothing hand on the wet neck. Patience and waiting would bring the next moves to him.

"You, what the hell you doing here?" The voice came

from above him and across the wall, harsh even in the distant thinness. Joe made no move but sat quietly, waiting on the bay.

Another shot started an echo, closer this time, just above his head, the closeness sending the bay dancing again, bringing the blue up on his hind legs. Joe eased the horses again and continued his stubborn silence.

It had to happen. The stillness of the clean air, the perfectness of the broken yellow rock, the hardness of the shelly ground, would have to be violated by the impatience of man. The guard appeared in front of Joe, a lean man with dark stubbled face and a squint to his right eye. He held up a rifle in silent question and waited for his answer. Just out of Joe's reach. Continued silence brought the man one step closer; anger forced another step. Growing impatience made him blunder.

Joe kicked out and caught the guard on the side of his jaw, the boot toe slicing along the stubble line and flicking across the man's eye. The blow dropped him instantly. As the bay sidestepped the fallen man, Joe leaned down and pulled the rifle out from under the body. The blue roan jumped the shadowed body and kicked out at the formless pile, his sharp hooves missing the humped shoulders. Joe snugged the blue back to his knee.

Then the bay settled to a walk, and Joe nodded as the familiar valley opened up before him. The trail slanted down again, then leveled out across the green perfection of the canyon. Memory had served him well, but there had been changes here over the missing years.

Up against the side wall, under the darkening of scrub pine, and hidden from unknowing eyes, was a cabin. Built with half-round logs, it was crude, basic shelter, enough in this godforsaken hideaway. A blackness in the front wall told Joe the door stood open, let him know someone was watching his trip across the canyon floor. He kneed the bay from the thin line that headed to the cabin and headed for the slow gathering of silent men near two corrals.

He would deal with these men, and then the leader would come to him. He spoke before halting the bay, his voice loud enough in the clear air to bring up heads and prick ears from the broncs milling in the pens.

"Your guard's got a sore head 'bout now. Two of you get out there; bring him in."

The command stirred two men into pushing away from the fence, then an awareness of the automatic reaction stopped them, tightened identical faces, put hands to gun butts. Joe carelessly let the guard's rifle come to rest on his thigh, hand cradled at the center, finger gently on the trigger.

"I said ride out and pick up that man. Another stranger could ride over him and be inside before you yahoos knew better. Get."

He knew it would work. The same two men picked up their slow-motion walk, sorted out gear, and saddled two horses. The men remaining held the silence, waiting out the rest of the bluff. Then the roan swung his head, ears pricked to touch. One man, younger than

98

the others, closer to the side wall, turned his head a fraction, shifted his eyes, then came back to watching Joe.

And Joe smiled down at him, dropping his head in acknowledgment. A flush of red came to the still-young face. Joe sat the bay, almost able to count the cushioned steps as the man walked up to stand just behind his line of vision. The bay shifted, and Joe held him steady.

"So you finally figured out someone else knew about your extra home." Joe spoke to the man without trying to see him. So close to knowing, he would not push; he would go slow and careful. He legged the bay sideways, blessing Stratmeyer for owning a good mount. The bay bumped into a solid shape, and Joe looked down to a familiar face. Ed Duncan's face.

He should have been surprised, but the fit was perfect. Duncan the brawler, Duncan the big, stupid man who took the orders and liked the work.

The big-shouldered man had to look up to met Joe's gaze, and the resentment was clear in his face. Admiration, too, as if Duncan knew Joe's moves and acknowledged their success.

Duncan nodded once at Joe's tipped head. He had stood in the cabin doorway to watch the deliberate ride across the floor, had watched when the two men rode out under orders. Good. Joe Gilead had come to him.

"You finally got here. Figured you'd end up here after that shootup with your daddy. What makes you figure on a welcome? Nobody but the law wants you, boy." The smooth voice bit hard into Joe.

But his recognition was complete; he knew Ed

Duncan now. Prison; the one big man who ruled the rest by cunning and brutality. He had not known Duncan, but each prison had its Duncan, and its corner of hell. Joe brought his stare back to the patiently waiting man.

"You're a clever son, knowing I'd ride in here. Leaving me an easy mark out there. I'm here 'cause I plan to take what's mine and ride the hell out. And you're going to help me take it."

"Ah, Joey boy. We don't need you. Got all the men we need here. Get out now while these men'll still let you go. There's nothing you can give we can't take."

It was Joe's now. The words came easily, planned on the long empty ride. "Took me less than half a day to find you, Duncan. You got just enough smarts to be in trouble."

He saw the truth hit Duncan and knew he was one step closer. But the big man tried a laugh.

"Think again, Gilead. We got our line to the ranchers; we know what they plan before they decide. You got nothing for us, mister, 'cepting a handgun and a hatred. We got plenty of them both."

Duncan saw too much and not enough. The two men took a slow measure of each other. And Duncan still had the edge. He pushed at Joe, wanting to own his knowledge but wary of taking him too quickly. There was something off in the man. Men like Gilead didn't stay on the wrong side of the law for long, even with seven years of prison behind them. Something got to them, made them dangerous to men like Duncan. But the man could be used.

So Duncan watched the rider carefully, saw the muscles jump along the jawline, felt the long fingers bunch and gather on his thigh, too near the high-riding handle of the pistol. Duncan waited; he could afford to wait. The men surrounding him took his lead and settled back, stood easy.

He learned that the seven years had taught Joe Gilead well. The man held his temper, eased the tightness that stiffened his back, and settled imperceptibly back into the saddle. Such discipline made the man even more dangerous. He held an ace, and Duncan knew the card would turn up soon, but he was willing to gamble, for he needed the knowledge.

Gilead's voice, when he finally broke the deadlock, was soft and polite, but his words dug into Duncan's self-esteem and found his weak point.

"You're a braggart, Duncan; you know nothing. Not the back trails, not the safe trails. Without me you'll never know."

Joe stopped, to fill his head with all the contempt and anger waiting inside him. The strength of his disdain gave the next words a driving force.

"Killing those punchers was a dumb move; got everyone against you now. Soon enough you won't be able to take a step in these parts without some puncher taking a shot at you. The taking's going to turn wicked, Duncan, and you'll lose your men and yourself unless you got something more. And that's me. Killing those men was stupid."

A long speech for the taciturn rider, a speech calculated to taunt his man and force him out. The men who circled Joe had listened to the biting words, and worry turned them to bring the circle closer, to question their boss. The big man's temper almost broke, but the staring faces kept him together. He hadn't lost yet.

So he looked up at the rider. He could put all his anger to this one man. Take him, use him, and kill him. So simple. Killing the two cowhands had been easy for Duncan; he saw their deaths as a joke on the righteous Stratmeyer, and an exercise of his own power. He knew now that the gesture had brought him immediate trouble, sitting a solid bay horse, right in front of him.

Gilead's quiet voice once again dug at the rawness in Duncan. "I'm that something more you need. I want in, want what's mine. And you'll help me get it. The rest I don't care about; it's yours for the taking."

The tight circle of men nodded almost in unison at the offer. The same words were a spur to Duncan, planted deep; the big man finally nodded but would not give more than that. He walked away from horse and rider, his exposed back enough to let his men know. For now, Joe Gilead was to be allowed in the canyon. The circle drifted apart, Joe brought his two horses to the corral, and slipped from the off side, careful to keep the horse between himself and the jagged groups of men.

The precaution was noted and approved. Joe off saddled the bay and turned the two horses loose in a pen, staying to watch them roll and then fight their way to a share of the loose-cut grass. He knew instantly when the three riders came to the camp, one man digging furiously at his sluggish horse, going straight for Duncan almost at the cabin door. The other two riders came in slowly, an easy pair headed to the corral, their chores completed.

The wild rider swung his lathered horse around Duncan, keeping him from the cabin door; a long lean rider, hatless, hands flying, face pale around a livid bruise that covered his jaw, rusted streaks lined from his nose and mouth. The words could not be heard, but the meaning of the short and violent exchange was obvious.

Duncan grew agitated, the circling horse came to a standstill, and then a big hand sent the rider sprawling from the sweated animal. The man came up fast but turned away from Duncan and remounted. He may have been dismissed, but his fury was alive and growing. The horse and rider came to the corrals at a gallop, stopping in a flurry of dust and gravel.

The man dismounted, found Joe leaning back against a rock, gear at his feet, horses quiet in the dusty-stirred pen, chewing automatically. A grimace came over the bruised face as Joe nodded once in mock salute, then turned his back to the man, slowly picked up his meager gear, adding to the insults already suffered.

Joe knew. He was in camp on sufferance and would have to answer for the swollen jaw and flaming eyes. He also knew Duncan would use him and kill him without thought. He eased his back into the hardness of his saddle and settled his hat down across his face. The lean, squint-eyed man did not count. Only Duncan, and the cattle, counted.

He stayed to himself. Not by choice, although he preferred his company to that of the men around him. No one picked a fight, no one forced a confrontation, but the grouping of men let Joe know he was suspect. It was a measure of Duncan's strength that he was allowed to stay unmolested. For all that he had served time, he was a rancher born, from the Resolution basin, and not one of this loose confederation of outlaws. The squint-eyed man made certain no one forgot.

He knew the peace would not last, that the lean outlaw had to regain his own respect. So he was not surprised when the challenge came.

The man stood over Joe as he reached for another cup of the bitter coffee. The long puncher with the nervous right eye carried a handgun this time and was backed by five more just like him. The bruise had faded, the rusted streaks washed away, but there was still a swelling on the long jaw and hatred in the restless eyes.

It was Joe's solitary fire, Joe's small pot of brewing coffee, that began the lesson.

"I'll have me that cup a coffee, you. Belongs to us that be here, not some fancy outrider. Give me that cup . . ."

The pure bitter smell of the dark liquid, the chatter of the hot fire, made it easy to ignore the intruding words. The man was too willing to talk, too slow to act. Talk softened a threat.

The man stood just above him, one foot resting close to Joe's hand, still caught in reaching for the pot handle. "You just hand me that cup right now; do just what I tells you." The foot moved back from the quick-burning fire; the voice above Joe came too loud. Joe's hand tightened on the handle, poured black liquid into the waiting cup, and moved it slowly back from the fire, his head down in seeming compliance with the order. He brought the cup partway to the reaching hand, still, slow, deliberate. Joe gathered himself, drew a deep breath, and his left hand came forward to reach behind the slightly bent knee and pull hard, at the same time throwing the hot brew and metal cup at the looming face. The thin body came down in the middle of the small fire, scattering the red coals, folding them into the man's shirt, rubbing them against his pants leg, raising welts on bared flesh. Short screams came from the downed man, cut off by a kick to his head that rolled him free from the fire and into unconsciousness.

Joe came fully erect with the murderous kick and stepped back from the prone body, sensing around him, searching for that one sound that would tell of the next attack. The fight had been too short. He looked for the challenge and found only eyes that were unwilling to meet his, heads turned away from the smoking body, watching instead something beyond Joe.

He picked up the pot and poured a line of the coffee onto the smoldering bits of clothing. His boot toe scattered the remains of the fire, and the pot made a

105

shocking sound as it hit rock and clattered from his throw. He had been set up. Duncan. This had come with his approval.

Joe turned and looked for the man. And found him leaning against a saddled horse, half-smoked butt loose in the fingers of one hand, reins to the stocky bay in the other. As Joe's eyes found him, the man straightened up, away from the support of the gray horse, and held out the split leather reins.

"Just waiting till Spence there got that out of his craw. Won't be at you again; no one will." The words were meant to reassure, but Joe knew the implied threat behind them. The attack would be final and would come from behind next time. Both men looked down at the fallen outlaw lying beyond the fire, arms spread wide in the dirt, blood seeping from behind his ear where Joe's boot had torn flesh.

"Yeah, he's stupid, that one. Always has been, but he do take orders and can hit what he aims for. Waited till I said to before tackling you. Didn't do him much good; didn't think it would. Take the bay. We got us some cattle to move. Got word last night."

Joe had heard the rider come in fast and leave late. The temptation to walk over near the small cabin and listen, find out the traitor, had been strong, but he knew this was not the time. He would never ride out of the small canyon if he showed any interest in the shadow man.

There were others saddled and ready to ride. Seven in all. Duncan mounted the smooth-muscled gray and motioned for Joe to ride up with him. The command was no surprise.

"You stay beside me, mister. Show me the trail, and ride off the cattle. Right beside me the whole way. Don't want you behind me, ever. We'll see, after today."

They would test him, and they would force him. Rustling, raiding against his own, would challenge him as Duncan knew it would. He needed to ride bold and willing into the work as if he wanted to come back and finish what he had put in motion.

Joe turned the bay and headed out of the small, safe canyon. Ed Duncan rode alongside him, one stride slower. Behind him five more silent men covered his back.

Chapter 12

W ayne Babson drew his hand fast across the protruding stone of the big fireplace, and an answering flame rose from the sulfur match. He brought the light to below his mouth and sucked in on the thick cigar, drawing a bright ash from its tip. Finally satisfied with the light, he dropped the match into the litter of the hearth and turned around to face the roomful of men. Old men mostly, ranchers who had been in this end of the Dakota land for a good many years, men who had worked together in the early days, then for many reasons separated into isolated ranches. He nodded his greeting to Evan Gilead, by a good many years the oldest man in the room. It was Evan's word that had brought them all to the meeting.

There were more than fifteen men in the cramped space, drawn by their individual concerns. The brutality of the murders up on High Top, the theft of the small herd, had the men on edge. Spring gather was coming up, and each man carried a deeply buried fear of rustling. They wanted to hear Gilead's words, knowing he had already been hit. Not a man in the room was surprised by the meeting's call so close to Mary's death and burial. They had all buried family somewhere and immediately turned to their work, to grieve in private. The band of men waited.

Matlock Glover, tightfisted and querulous, had a small grouping around his chair, listening to him complain about the effort it had taken for him to be here. Damn, the meetings took up too much of a man's time. Always too much to do.

And Winchell Potter, thinned to a pole by illness, a bitter shine to his eyes; he'd already challenged Evan outside at the big door, questioning him to no use about all the "secret" ideas that called for this gathering.

Evan Gilead had been the leader for a long time, a well-respected man, a successful man. But the tragedy of his sons, the death of his beloved wife, well, the man could be addled by the shame and the loss. Even those who knew Evan well, such as Warren Smithson and Charlie Haines, they, too, were beginning to question the soundness of Evan's leadership. They were willing to listen this one last time, but the doubt in the room had a life of its own. Evan stood at the doorway only for a moment and felt the tension run its circle.

He spoke before settling in the hard-backed chair. "I know you boys got questions, but that don't change a durned thing. You got to wondering about the good common sense that God might of left me with these last months. Well, don't fret, I still know a mare from a gelding." The raspy voice startled the murmuring groups, causing some of the more doubtful to flinch. It was as if he had read their thoughts.

"My wife's dead, my boys gone. But I still got a ranch and mean to keep it till I die. If any of you want to give up to them rustlers, then you up and ride out. Then the rest of us will know our friends, who we count on." No one stirred. They waited, hardly daring to breathe, wondering if one person would leave.

Back in his corner, isolated by his whiskey temper, Hardin Fowler knew the old man looked right at him with the challenge. But the old man couldn't know, couldn't guess, the name of the traitor. Fowler sat up straighter, looked around the small room, careful to avoid the glancing eyes of his father-in-law. It had been Hardin's plan to one day live in this house, but those plans were changing. The invite to come to the meeting had fitted right in with his new ideas. So he sat in his corner and spoke to no one, content to listen.

Gilead continued: "You all getting ready to gather up stock and cut, brand, cull. This time we do it together. No more of this bickering we been doing the past years. Put all our men together, have us a big gather, near the basin. We can push the stock into Blackman's canyon, big enough to hold the whole damned Dakotas. If we band together, them rustlers won't be able to pick off the nice small herds we've been putting out for them." He had to stop: the volume of small words spoken to each neighbor cut into the carrying sound of his voice, drowning him in the questions and doubts.

Snow Dunning ran a hand through his crown of white hair and spoke up real loud, strong enough to silence the mutterings. Heads turned at his question. "You got this all lined out, Evan, or you figured to have us argue here all night picking men and pushing at one another?"

Evan smiled at the old friend; he knew he could count on Dunning. "Yep, got it all figured. You settle down and listen; wait till I'm done, then complain and curse all you likes. Did some figuring, and some talking. Watson and McCormick over near Stone Mountain, they want in, got some winter spread beefs over this way and see the big gather as bringing them back easy. Rose, too, down beyond the badland, he's been hit by these damned rustlers. Just never let us know.

"Need a remuda of two, three hundred broncs. Each of you throw in what you got. Twenty-five, thirty men ought to keep us going. I got a cook wagon; Coombs already offered his. Figure Stratmeyer here to boss the job. Set up crews of five, six men; have two main camps—one near the badlands, other up to Medora. That way we can pick up all the strays, and Blackman's close enough to drive small herds easy. They's only one way in to Blackman's, and we'll set up a guard, good men knowing their job. Keep them rustlers off our backs this time. Got any problems?"

Hardin Fowler jumped at the numbers—maybe ten thousand or more, thousands more than Duncan could handle. There had to be a way to get that herd. His share would be enough to make him kingpin in the basin, especially since the other ranchers would be flattened by the theft. He'd add his pitiful stock to the gather, send his men and horses, and then wait for Duncan to do the work. There had to be a way to get at the riches being set up for him.

Dunning's strong voice dominated: "Evan, it's a good plan but you sure Stratmeyer can handle the setup?" He did not bother to look at the foreman as he spoke the damning words. Evan would know.

"Snow, John here's got the knowledge, can handle the men. It's a matter of strategies, and he's sure good at keeping things moving." What went unspoken between Dunning and Gilead, what kept John Stratmeyer quiet, was the unavenged deaths on High Top. Those two bodies would ride with Stratmeyer, push him beyond himself to hold the men and horses together, to dig out all the stock, pen it in Blackman's, and guard it from the thieves. Stratmeyer's guilt would be his taskmaster.

Snow nodded at the words and glanced around the room. All these cowmen had burdens, some way in the past, that rode them every day. They would accept Stratmeyer as boss. Babson barely looked at Snow, spending most of his time staring at the end of the blunted cigar. Smithson and Haines already were counting horses, picking and choosing men for the gather. The rest would follow.

The two women met three miles outside the crossroads called Resolution. It took Lucy a moment to place the young woman mounted on the small bay mare. Young, straight, with fine blond hair and a clean manner, she sat the well-bred mare and offered a cautious smile. Lucy placed her now—the young woman who had walked beside the old man at the funeral.

Elissa had not met the worn woman on the rough-seated farm wagon. She had seen her several times, the funeral, in town, and knew the local gossip. But she did not know the woman. A glimpse of the lined face, the roughened hands, and Elissa pitied her without thinking, without knowing, that she could become the same in only a few years.

They exchanged smiles, eager with the plains woman's loneliness to enjoy companionship. Lucy patted the hard seat, and Elissa slipped from the mare in one step to sit down in the tilted wagon. The mare tied easily behind, and the lame gray pulled them toward the barren buildings of Resolution. Introductions came and went, and the women chatted the miles, words overlapping as they tried to cover everything in the short time.

They parted at the narrow building that served as the circuit courthouse and church and housed the doctor at the top of the outside line of stairs. Elissa waited to watch Lucy climb the steps, stopping every third one for a quick breath. Then she led the mare to the one other building, the combined general store and cavernous bar. At this time of day the connecting door would be closed, and it would be safe and proper for a woman to enter the store side to shop.

Even as she raised her hand to knock on the thin paneled door, Lucy hoped the doctor would not be in, that he would not be there to tell her what she did not want to know. That she was pregnant. After eight years of marriage to a man she did not love, she was pregnant.

But the door opened under her raised fist, and the round and boyish face of Edgar Travers showed its surprise and delight even as she took one step back.

Elissa finished her small chores at Stillman's. Canned milk was the bulk of the awkward parcel she tied behind the cantle. The foal had survived the first few days of its life, and she was committed now to seeing it through the next few months until it could eat grain and hay. Every time she looked at the pitiful thing, wobbling painfully on the letdown tendons and loosened joints, she heard Joe Gilead's voice telling her it was a kindness to let it die.

And she remembered her retort—that even the worst deserves a chance. She thought of him, of his face and the twist that crossed it as she spoke. She could see him, somewhere out beyond the good Resolution basin land, riding with the thieves and murderers on his stolen horse. Perhaps it was a kindness to let maimed things die.

Then she would kneel to touch the foal, stroke the

pale yellow coat, and watch the tired baby sink to the soft bedding of straw. The harsh judgment would be suspended by the foal's continued struggle to live.

The Fowler wagon was still in front of the doctor's long stairway. Elissa tied her mare and quickly mounted the steps to knock at the door, seeking company on part of the long ride back to the Three V. Even in the dim light she knew she was an intruder, that these two were trying to deal with something in which she had no part. But before she could retreat, Lucy Fowler looked at her, and the panic was easy to read. Elissa smiled at the woman, a timid smile meant to encourage.

"Mrs. Fowler, I just came to see if you'd like company on the ride back. I could wait downstairs if you would like." A gentle invitation, meant to be polite and neighborly, nothing more. And Elissa was surprised as Lucy rose abruptly without answering and bolted past her to the stairs. She stumbled at the top step, caught herself, and then went down the stairs quickly, hands skipping along the railing in support. Elissa followed, after looking one more time at the puzzled face of the doctor.

Without question she sat on the hard seat and picked up the reins to her mare as the gray walked in a slow, wide arc that would turn them out of the small square. She saw the doctor stand at the top of his long stairs, not moving, not protesting, but standing silhouetted in the narrow framed door.

"I can't stay with Hardin; I can't. He'll destroy this

child as surely as he's destroyed me. I won't do that, even to his own child."

The words were a shock. Elissa looked at the speaker; Lucy was rigid on the wagon seat, eyes straight ahead, hands barely closed on the clumsy leather lines. Elissa drew up a hand to touch the drawn-up shoulders, soothe the anger away, but Lucy stiffened from the proffered comfort. The short and damning monologue hung between the two women, the bitter words raising sorrow and a touch of admiration for the rail-thin woman. Elissa's offer came without thought, without caution.

"Come live with us, with my father and me, and Mr. Gilead. I'm alone on the ranch; there's lots of room. You'd be welcome, I know. Please, come live with us."

Lucy's hands slipped their hold on the reins. The gray felt even that slight loss and stopped, grateful for a chance to rest. Lucy turned to the young woman beside her and looked carefully into the clear eyes. The offer was real, and life-giving. A tentative smile shaped her face into a touch of beauty.

"Thank you, oh, yes. I'll come and stay. Thank you. I'll live with you, at least for a while. But I won't go back to get anything until I know Hardin won't be there. I couldn't face him yet."

The old wagon was quiet, creaking only as one of the passengers shifted on the uncomfortable seat. Wind caught at the edge of loose hair, tugging at the blond braid and freeing the tightly bound dark curls. Then the older woman, face lined, eyes hollow and darkened, smiled. One work-reddened hand sought out a softer, smoother, younger one, and then the gray felt the familiar tightening on the reins, a flick of a whip across his sloping rump, that started him walking again. This time, as he turned by long habit to the grass-covered track to the Wagon Wheel, a firm hand guided him back to the main road, to the longer curved miles that would bring horse and wagon to the quiet, safe valley of the Three V.

Chapter 13

The ride through the breaks was short and silent. The seven men rode single-file, no smokes, no small talk, only the occasional jingle of a spur or creak of a dry saddle to speak of their passage. Joe kept the bay to an easy jog, threading him through the narrow path. Eyes up, he kept checking, waiting to find the odd mark high up on the wall that would lead the men beyond the simple trail they rode.

Duncan's low cursing could almost be heard. He rode behind Joe, his heavy gray bumping the wide rump of the bay, mirroring his rider's impatience. The trail was unfamiliar to Duncan; his cursing grew louder.

But Joe knew. There was a thin wedge of rock broken from the steep wall, wide enough to allow horse and rider behind it up the side of the slanted wall, away from the badlands and nearer to the small grassy basin holding prime stock waiting to be lifted.

The short hairs at his neck itched as he heard the man

riding too close behind him, and the others following him, each with his hand never straying from the comforting touch of a handgun, each with a rifle jammed deep in the scabbard under one leg. The quick-rising trail took the men out to a wide and familiar grassland, but they were at the far end of the expanse, away from the window sights of the small, crude house. The main trail, the one legitimate riders used daily, was distinctive in its brown line winding among the brightness of the spring greening.

Joe put the bay to a slope down a long swale in the heavy grass, then made a sweeping turn right that brought the riders up another slope, right to the edge of a brush-lined graze. He could sense Duncan's horse come alongside the bay, and did not turn but only tilted his head to the faint line down the far side and waited.

"You better be damned sure where you got us heading, Gilead. We don't take to this open ground."

Joe kept watching straight ahead, looking for an old and stunted pine, one of the few in the vast area. The bay snorted and sidestepped as Duncan's gray tried to come abreast. The big gray was forced back to follow at wide quarters as Joe kept to the edge of the brush. The riders jammed into one another, eased their horses, and settled back into their order.

The land bunched and turned quickly from good graze to more upended rock and thinning soil. Scrub bush thickened, trapping the horses' legs. Joe rode parallel to the densest scrub, then drove the bay into the tangle. The blocky horse jumped the first line of brush, then skittered through the woven scrub. The other riders hesitated, leery of the blind jump, then gigged their horses into the forbidding mass, following Joe's lead.

He eased the jarring of the bay's trot by standing erect, with his weight deep in the stirrups, one hand for balance on the swell. He kept the horse weaving fast through the tightly packed bushes. There was a faint path if a rider could stop to sight it. The rise of brush absorbed all outside sound until all Joe could hear was the grunt of his horse's labored breathing and the scrabble of small branches against the heavy leather protection of his gear. The horses climbed in the silence, riders leaning with them, ducking constantly from the snap of sharpened twigs against their exposed skin.

The bay stopped suddenly. The trail widened out over the crest of a steep slope. Six men fanned out beside Joe and reined in tired mounts. The animals lowered their heads and snorted, blowing with the exertion, leather popping from heaving sides.

"You never did say where we was headed, Duncan. I brought you to Blackman's. Backside of the basin, old trail lost years ago. No cattle down there now, mister. You just taking us out for a ride, or did you have some place special in mind?"

Duncan didn't mind the caustic words; barely even registered their meaning. What lay below him was a treasure. Old Joey Gilead had already paid his way.

From Blackman's they could fan out, take the small outlying ranches, and drive the cattle back through the fan-shaped basin. It would take a long time and a great many tracks before a path would show through the lush-growing grasses below him.

But he didn't need months; he'd had enough of this petty thieving. This time, this one last time, he was going to pick up a good number of the spring gathers and split. The word was out, and more men were heading to the hidden canyon. When there were enough, and when the ranchers had placidly begun their spring chores, then he would strike and take what he wanted. And the knowledge of the back exit from Blackman's would be his edge.

He heard more words beside him and nodded absently without speaking. Gilead was beside him, saying something. Duncan sent his gray over the rim, where the faint markings of the old trail were still visible. The spurs dug deep into the gray sides carried horse and rider far down the slope in one leap. Startled horses and riders milled uncertainly, but only for a moment, then the remaining rustlers followed Duncan's lead. Joe thought to hold back, but a dusty hat slapped on the bay's rump put the horse running down the incline, catching Duncan just as the big man lined his gray out along the wide basin at a run. Then Duncan pulled in on the gray and once again stationed himself just behind Joe Gilead's left shoulder. The two horses kept a steady gallop, the other five men strung out behind them.

The basin narrowed to a slender mouth, then opened again to the flowing swell of the grasslands. Duncan's gray edged Joe and the bay to the right, and the men soon hit a well-traveled trail. The horses slowed to a trot, and Duncan wordlessly guided the small group to a slow rise in the endless prairie.

Almost dark, almost too dim to see cattle below, heads busy in the lush grass pulling at the short stalks, jaws going sideways in constant motion. Duncan reined in the gray and stopped Joe with a cautious, quiet word. The men sat and looked down at the small bunching of cows. Just waiting there to be rounded up and go for a short walk that would put hard cash in the rustlers' pockets. Duncan grinned, and the white of his teeth was just visible.

"Here's your big chance, Gilead. We take them cattle and drive back up to the river. Won't go near Blackman, though; don't want no nosy cowhand finding out what we know. Yet. That'll come soon enough. You ride, now."

Down the slope and on flat ground, the five men split and made a wide loop to circle the cattle, then spun their horses and started the herd moving. Joe rode to one side, Duncan close behind him. There was a quick flash at the far end of the shallow basin, a shot echoing overhead, and a horse came into view. Joe hauled in the bay and turned into Duncan's gray. Duncan cursed in sputtering anger and looked up to see the horseman. Three steers bolted past the two riders, fleeing the confusion. Joe sat and watched them go.

"Gilead, get them steers. We ain't leaving nothing behind." The voice was loud over the bellowing confusion. The horse and rider too close. Then the steers ran into the single horse and rolled the animal, the rider sailing clear. Head tucked to shoulder in blind instinct, the puncher turned twice before sprawling on the ground. The paint struggled to stand, and the three steers continued their panicked run.

Then the rider sat up and looked straight at Joe. Recognition was already there. Duncan had seen to that with his yelling. Joe shifted the bay to look into the big man's face and saw the smug grin lining the heavy mouth. He sat the big gray quietly in the milling herd and yelled again.

"To hell with them steers now, Gilead. Too late. Get going." Then he turned his back on Joe and the motionless puncher and ran the gray down the depression, catching up quickly with the rustlers and the madly spinning herd. In a close group horses and cattle hit the slope and bucketed to the top, not pausing for breath, but streaming down the easy rim out onto the wide plains.

The downed rider made no move but continued to stare at Joe. The faint sound of another horse came to them both, and Joe swung the bay around to catch the laboring gray at the far side of the rise. He had to lean sideways to be sure Duncan heard him, but the anger let him take the chance.

"You won, Duncan; now the whole basin knows." He got a wide grin in return, and Joe saluted him. Duncan was a clever son. He'd pulled Joe in neatly and set him up not to back out.

Then Duncan whirled the gray and fired at two men mounted on a single horse, struggling to hit the top of the rise. One shot came close enough to graze the tired dun, and the horse spun around under the double burden, crazed from the stinging pain. The riders leaned with the turn, but the second man bounced off after two bucking strides and left his companion to deal with the enraged horse. The man stood slowly, picked up his hat, and watched the last of the cattle disappear.

They were back just before dawn, tracks buried in the miles of rocky trails, horses salted white with sweat. A success—only a few shots fired, no one touched. One horse had broken a leg, so two men returned double. And now Joe Gilead was recognized as riding with the thieves. The word would go back to the rest of the basin. And his father. That gave Duncan a stronger faith in the man, but even with this extra protection, Gilead was his only for a short while. He would sicken and go back to his kind.

The big man's smile grew. He wanted the fight with this man, a fight to finish the one started at the Three V ranch that day. He saw in Joe Gilead a worthwhile opponent. There was pleasure in battling a man for hard cash, a drive that money brought to the contest. This battle would have the Resolution basin as its purse.

As the riders followed in the dust of the small herd, a new set of riders appeared, on fresh horses, handkerchiefs wrapped to filter the dust. They would move the herd to a buyer already waiting over the border. Duncan watched as the last rider disappeared, then swiveled in the saddle.

Below him a big fancy sorrel horse was tied to a tree just outside the small cabin. So, Hardin Fowler was in camp. There would be an interesting meeting between Fowler and the newly recruited rustler. Duncan rode to the cabin and scowled down at the sleeping figure just outside the door.

Joe turned the bay loose and stood for a moment longer. The tiredness came back in multiplied strength, loosening his thighs, numbing his mind. He watched the bay as the horse lay down and rolled in a depression, sending puffs of dust up as his legs pushed into the soft ground in an attempt to roll over. Finally satisfied, the chunky bay stood and shook with a long sigh, then turned and snapped at a nosy black. In moments the bay was asleep, knees locked, head low, tail slapping occasional pests.

Joe kept his thoughts on the bay, envying the simple wants and easy solutions. He was a thief now. Once a murderer, and now a thief. He had Duncan's limited trust, which would not last. The trade for his self-esteem had little value. He knew the end to what he was doing, but the night's work still ate at him, twisting his belly to fire.

He saw a man step up to talk with Duncan. A familiar shape, one from a long way back. Then the man walked to a big sorrel that was not a camp horse. Joe moved closer to the cabin and the tied sorrel. The man continued talking to Duncan even as he fiddled with his cinch and untied the fancy horse. The head turned at the sound of Joe's footsteps, and the two stared at each other over the shortened distance. Joe covered his tracks by wiping at the sweat and dust streaking his face, then retying the bandanna around his neck. The face stayed in front of him.

Hardin Fowler. Duncan's line to the ranchers. The turncoat. Joe only nodded with indifference and walked beyond the two men as if in a definite direction.

Fowler turned quickly to Duncan, in his panic not seeing the grin hovering on Duncan's mouth. "What the hell is this, Ed? Why've you got Gilead walking around here? The goddamn fool's a threat. He knows now I'm connected to you. Goddamn it, Ed."

He ran out of words and finally had to listen. Duncan's voice was pitched low and soothing, as if speaking to a frightened child. "Nothing to worry you, Hardin. Joe here belongs to us now. Rode on a raid already; them cattle you told us about. And you'll be hearing that the old man lost more. Best part, one of his men saw this pretty son of his riding right along with us thieves. Nice, ain't it. But nothing to worry you about, Hardin. There ain't nothing this man's going to do to you."

The words didn't quiet Hardin. The man's face turned a darker red as he watched Joe and tasted the memory of his defeat in Stillman's. The boy had grown more like Hank, even more like his daddy. The solid shoulders, the long muscles. But there was a set to his eye that was not like Hank. This Gilead was a threat to him. Another goddamn Gilead. Just the thought fueled his anger. Lucy. Left him by god without a note and living with the Gileads. Them Gileads had taken too much from him, and now another one stood in front of him, knowing too much. This Gilead was going to die.

It had been too easy for Joe to read the thoughts raging through Fowler as he took his slow walk by the man. Everything inside him wanted to pummel the man, to beat the weak face into a pulped mass. He kept the reaction from showing. Duncan was watching. He willed himself quiet, nodded indifferently to the traitor, to Duncan, and walked away. Very slowly, as if nothing mattered except firewood for hot coffee and a quick breakfast.

It almost worked. Except that the meeting fitted in too nicely with Duncan's slow-forming plans. Fowler had brought word that the ranchers were planning a big spring gather at Blackman's canyon. The trail they'd ridden last night took them right to the canyon rim. Easy as pie. It might have been better to have Gilead lead, but not now, not with him knowing about Hardin Fowler. It would take only one mistake for the man to turn, and the surprise would be lost.

"That there son of a bitch purely hates you, Hardin. See it in his eyes. Give you odds he takes a stab at you somehow. Be just his style to get word to his old man about you being here. You got a problem."

He enjoyed watching the panic rise in Fowler. So

easy. Turn one loose on the other. Gilead was the weak link now, and Fowler could take care of that. Make the man feel good, tie him tighter to Duncan.

"Tell you what, Hardin. You finish up mounting that fancy horse and get running. Give me some time, and I'll send Gilead on the trail with an errand. You pick your spot and be waiting. This dead Gilead won't be missed."

Chapter 14

Track Williams hadn't lasted all these years by accident. He hollered at Utah. The top of the banking, where he could still see dust settling and dark shapes of riders, was a perfect spot to leave a man behind with a shotgun, to wait for two dumb cow nurses to play hero and ride up that hill. In the quick-coming dark, heroes would be clay pigeons. Track hadn't reached the solid and respectable age of fifty-three by being dumb.

He might be no hero, and he might be setting on the ground cursing that paint, but he knew his horses, and his men. And he surely had recognized Mr. Stratmeyer's blocky bay with the high points and crooked blaze. He knew the rider instantly; it hadn't been needed for the big man to yell out a name. Hell, even Utah seen who it was, and the man had a real slow way of figuring things.

Track had ridden the tough Dakota lands for the Three V coming to more than thirty years now, starting up with the old man months after he'd settled the small valley with them two sons and the wife. The baby came two years later. A good family that had become his family.

He shook his bald head in painful memory, and Utah, as usual, misread the sign. "Goddamn thieving bastards, I be sure to shooting I saw Joe Gilead riding with them sons. That there herd was good stuff. I never heard no talk about a trail headed up there. Figured it was too thick in that damnable brush. That Gilead son of a bitch knows this land sure better'n us, Track. That murdering son, his old man . . ."

The words went on, and Track could do nothing but agree. First they had to pick up the paint. Poor beginning to a cow horse's career, getting run down by the spiteful critters. He straightened and started for the paint, talking to Utah over his shoulder. "You hit back for the Dunning spread; tell the word. I'm riding to the old man. He sure ain't going to like this piece of news any more than I like telling it."

Utah straightened in the saddle, walking his horse alongside the older man. "Now that I think about it, it had to be the Gilead kid. Stole that crooked faced bay from Stratmeyer, not too long past. Ain't that right, Track?"

Utah failed to see the despair that crossed Track's burned face. There would be no easing the news now; Utah had a big mouth and a loose brain to match, and a wide range of cronies that would take their pleasure from today's happenings. Track shook his head again and looked up at the younger man, as if his silent command would pierce the thick skull of his riding companion. He could do nothing to stop Utah from riding away from him, heading toward the open graze and the Dunning ranch.

"You speak out what you want, Utah. Me, I know the old man got enough after him, and I ain't looking to run home with another tale. But you say what you want."

The unspoken plea passed right by Utah, and the man grinned at the morose face below him. Track Williams may be a good hand, a top hand, but be damned if the ranny weren't getting some age and losing his brains along with his hair. Utah kicked the dun and jogged for a few strides, trying for a casual departure. Then natural exuberance and a relief at being still alive got to him and he spooked the horse into a wild run with a yell and a hat slapped alongside the dark shoulder.

Track held tight, and the paint half reared against the reins, then came down. He mounted and pushed the horse to a trot. The Three V trail would come soon enough. He knew he best get right to the old man, didn't want him hearing the wild and high-flying tale that would come a-roaring around soon as Utah hit the Dunning spread and got talking. Just the bare facts of the raid would drive the knife in deeper.

The ride back was cold, dark, and unfriendly. Track convinced himself he could wait till morning, that no one would be racing in to spread the word. He finally hit the home yard and sighed deep and long. The big Old Man, the one sitting above watching all the foolishness below, wasn't going to give Track a breather on this one. As he hit the yard, there was Mister Evan Gilead, sitting at the top of the veranda, wrapped in a heavy coat, silent as usual as the big rocker went back and forth real slow.

It was tempting not to see the hand wave him over, but Track wasn't clever enough to deceive. The old man wanted him right now, and Track sure enough had a reason to see him. He turned the paint to the steps, cursing the horse's light-colored streaks.

"Back early, Track? Never knew you to leave a job 'fore it's done. Something going on I need to know?"

Damn the old man for being so smart. Wasn't even going to give him a chance to lead to the mess. Damn.

"Mr. Gilead, they come down the back end of the canyon and took that herd right out from me and Utah. Never saw them till they had them critters running full-flight up the backside of the hill. There sure must of been a trail up there we didn't know 'bout, for them cattle disappeared like a magic trick. Utah and me, we figured not to follow. They was six, seven, men, and not scared of shooting; let us have a couple of quick ones to set us back. Worked. We took the hint. Utah's hit for the Dunning spread, and I came home. But that ain't the worst."

He knew the next words would be hard, but another look at the tough old man bent halfway round in his rocker, face stilled, listening and waiting, and he had to finish. This was a tough old man who'd lived through some tough years. And now he, Rutherford "Track" Williams, had more to add.

129

"Knew one of the horses, and the rider. Was Mr. Stratmeyer's bay, the one Joe stole. And Joe on it. Be hard for me to miss that set to him, but another man, big man, face covered, yelled out his name. As if he wanted me to know. That one was familiar, but I didn't get a set on him. I'm mighty sorry, Mr. Evan."

Track had to stop, wanted to turn the paint and ride out of the yard, ride almost anywhere that would take him away from the pained face setting right up in front of him. But he could only sit the tired horse and watch his boss.

Evan had known, almost as soon as Track had ridden in. The puncher never could hide anything, and one look at the burned and balding face, the despair right there to read in the pulled mouth and sagging eyes, and Evan had known. Something to do with Joe, something more.

As he listened, a surprised burst of relief came over him at the words of treachery. At least Joe was alive, not gunned down by a lawman or an eager hand working the spring gather. And he was still in the Resolution basin. There was still a chance.

"Track, you pick yourself a fresh horse, get over to Medora, and find that deputy. Sorry 'bout the long night ride, but this one can't wait. There ain't much he'll do about the lost herd, but he needs to know we're hard hit down here. Two herds in less than one month. Mighty rank. And Track, you take your time coming back. I hear there's a lady up to the high rim who sometimes misses your company. Get going."

130

Track Williams stood for one moment longer in front of the veranda. Admiration flooded him as he inspected the crooked figure of the old man. Give him tough news, stab him in the back with his own son's knife, and the old man comes back with a chance for Track to visit a certain lady. He reined the paint to the corral and knew deep inside he would die for this old man.

Track had to be wrong. Joe. But Joe had taken the bay. From all the horses I would give him on this ranch, he took that bay. Hank's death almost was easier, cleaner. Could put the blame somewhere, youth, liquor, rage. But this. Cold stealing from his kin, from folks he grew up with. Joe. What happened to you in that prison that changed you?

You were the best one, boy. You were the one carrying our hopes, holding our dreams. You were the one to stop and wonder, to reach for something you did not understand. Your brothers were loved, but you were the best. What happened in that damnable prison?

Evan Gilead closed his eyes and squeezed his hands hard into fists. The aged fingers and joints flared with the tension. He willed the pain to spread, to take him over and drive away the knowledge of his son's betrayal. He could see the face of Joe Gilead, standing mute before the judge, hearing his life finished by the words, sentenced to seven years of hell.

And he could remember how the words, the sentence, the hard voice of the judge, had hammered the strength from that erect figure, had dropped a weight on those broad shoulders that had broken them.

The newer, harsher face of Joe Gilead came to him, covering the image of that youth, leering at him through the network of scars and the deep lines of anger. The unknown and familiar face of a thief.

But that face still was his. Even with the rustling, Joe was his son; the blood never changed. And Evan loved him, wanted him home. The old man shuddered once, his body shaking with a torment. How he missed Mary, missed the comfort of her hand on his shoulder, her fingers stroking his face.

Instead of finding her beside him, he stood slowly and made his way inside, to the office. John Stratmeyer was still at work and needed to know of the theft. Something had to be worked out that would protect them all from Joe Gilead. The spring gather must continue.

Chapter 15

Hardin Fowler ran. He dug spurs into the big sorrel and let the horse run full out. The gelding was still in the first burst of speed when Hardin found his courage and hauled in on the heavy curb, drawing the big horse in a rear. He settled the animal at a lope and rode easy for a while, searching out the tumbled walls for the right spot.

He had come out from his ranch before dawn, armed with a shotgun and a line to the weary punchers sitting for their meal that he was hunting fresh meat for supper.

The story was thin, but no one cared enough to challenge him.

The lie complicated things now. The right spot had to be close to the trail, close enough to insure that the shotgun blast would destroy its target. And it had to be far enough back that he would not be exposed to the careful eyes of Joe Gilead.

The trail curved, and the sides narrowed for several strides, then opened wide along the river for a short distance. A good spot to water a horse after the dry ride from the canyon. Hardin let the sorrel have a drink while his eyes ranged the walls, checking the tumbled rocks for the right combination.

Three large boulders rested against one another, with a small scattering of rocks fallen across a pale gray ledge. A twisting of pine gave some shade to the backside of rock, and there was plenty of room to tie the sorrel out of sight and wait for a rider to stop and water his tired horse.

Hardin led the sorrel carefully across the pitted ledge, put a neck rope on the sweaty horse, and tied his dampened bandanna around the wet muzzle. A nicker from one lonesome horse to another would ruin the ambush.

And then he waited. This was the difficult time for him. He did not take to waiting; he wanted it all to come to him. He had never waited for anything much in his life, except for Lucy. But he was willing to sit now for that one rider to come down the narrow trail and stop to water a tired horse at the swirling shallow pool.

One more dead man, one more raid on the ranchers,

and Hardin Fowler would have what he wanted. He squirmed against the hard rock beneath his soft butt and thought of a smoke, a bottle, and a redheaded girl over the line in Montana. All in their time, after this dead man came down the trail right to him.

The bay was hot and tired. And Joe was reluctant. This fool errand of Duncan's was one he could not refuse; it had to be a test. So he saddled the bay very slowly and headed back out of the small, cool canyon into the dry heat of the closed-in track. Damn fool thing, a letter to be left with Fowler. Only Joe knew the land well enough to get up to the ranch and not be seen.

The bay stumbled, and Joe felt a brief pity. The roan had cast a shoe, so the bay had to make another trip. A drink would help, and he knew a pool was coming up at the widening of the walls. Instinct made him rein in the bay. They could both feel the cold water's freshness, could taste its teasing pleasure on the soft wind. The bay felt the air and whickered softly, tugging at the bit, eager for the drink.

But there was something wrong. Something Joe did not trust ahead. He sat the bay for more than ten minutes, testing, listening, waiting for what did not belong. The bay stamped his feet in impatience, then gave up and dropped his head to doze in the growing heat.

There was nothing. Joe edged the bay out of the security of the walls and into the open, then allowed the horse to drop his head completely into the cold water. He wanted to hurry. There was something that nudged at his back, pricked his instincts. He wiped at the sweat pooling in his collar, and the red cloth slipped from his greasy hand, clinging briefly to his pants, then sliding farther down to catch on the top of his boot.

He leaned down to grab the bandanna just as the booming echo of a shotgun came to him, just as a tearing force blasted him in the back, tearing long furrows in his neck and shoulders. He was thrown forward to cling to the black-maned neck that came up suddenly underneath his weight.

The bay leaped with the sound, stumbled as he went deeper into the river. Joe held to the slippery neck, aware only of the brand burning across his back. The horse turned in the stream, forced to swim with the flow of the water, desperate to be free of the clinging burden.

Then the horse tripped, and Joe lost his hold on the wet neck. Arched against the paralyzing pain, his body rolled from the saddle and went under the deepening water. The horse shied back and came out of the water to find the trail. He ran sideways, head high, careful to avoid the trailing reins, running against years of training, and running fast, to get away from the still-echoing sounds.

Hardin Fowler grinned as he watched horse and rider struggle in the spinning water. He could see the redness spread over the back of Gilead's shirt, going quickly from collar to belt line, down along his pants leg. The man was dead as he rode with the floundering horse. His body finally rolled from the high saddle and sank immediately in the faster-moving current. A few more moments of watching, and Hardin stood up to salute the death of Joe Gilead.

The cold wouldn't let go. The river tumbled him, bounced him along its sides, slamming him over roughened rocks, pushing him into the muddy bottom. Just as the air left his lungs, he would bob up into the false brightness of the sun and gulp one more time, then be drawn back into the cold green mass.

The river turned frantic, narrowed through steep walls that did not give it enough room for its power. The water was angry and white-capped as it flowed over the projecting rocks. Joe rode with the power, spun around by its force, numbed to uncaring by its coldness.

The funnel gave way to another widening place in the river where the waters slowed, the banks receded, and grasses and small trees grew along the shore. The lazy force moved Joe gently now, washing him in circles to the shallow sides.

His body bumped against a rotted tree rooted in the banking. The water continued beyond him, washing him in an easy rhythm up under the half-submerged tree. The bumping became even softer as he was so slowly pushed to the shoreline. Sand ground against the raw flesh of his face brought him awake. He could almost count the crystal-hard grains. He crawled forward until his head rested on the blessed green of river grass, and then his eyes closed again.

Something tickled his face. Joe fought to come awake, to come back from the tantalizing numbness of the cold river. His eyelids fluttered open, and he heard a soft snort. A black muzzle was close to him; yellowed teeth cropped at the thin grass near his eye. The head moved away, trailing a damp line of leather.

The bay gelding. The river. A shotgun blast. Joe tried to sit up and gagged at the pain through his back. He was lying on the pain, burying it deeper in his flesh. He struggled to roll over, and the bay head moved even farther away. The end of the rein was just out of reach.

On his belly the fire eased. The river numbness still held him, forcing him to move slowly. His mind fought to think, but blind instinct told him to move, and move fast. The horse. He had to secure the horse. That end of leather being jerked away from him was his lifeline.

One arm came up and away from his body, fierce pain pulling across his shoulders with the motion. His searching hand found the bit of stiff leather and held tight. The bay head came up against the restraint and pulled back. Joe could feel his hand, then his arm, then his whole body being drawn with the motion. The pain doubled, demanding he release the rein and let the arm drop back, let the fire burn out. The pain promised to leave if he let go.

He held out; the bay head came back down to the pressure. The arm dropped; the hand stayed tight around the thin leather. Joe's eyes closed against the insistent pounding across his back, and his mind fought an inviting blackness.

The warmth of the spring sun dismissed the cold, and blood began to ooze from the tiny holes across his back.

Long lines of blood dotted to his shoulders from a shot that had traveled the distance through flesh. The washing from the river had cleansed the wounds and closed some of the more shallow holes, but the blood was released by the sun.

The bay sighed and shook his head against an irritating fly. The rein tugged in Joe's hand. Without thinking, he drew his knees under him and pushed up, backside raised, shoulders still buried in the ground. The bay snorted at the strange shape and then settled, too tired to care.

Joe had thought a long time about what he was to do next. He made the move and was on his hands and knees, the rein still in one closed fist, then balanced precariously on his knees.

Finally he stood, staggered to the bay, and leaned on the well-trained horse. Then with effort he lifted his foot into the hanging stirrup, each move an exaggeration, each tensing of muscle a stabbing pain. He grabbed for the horn, and the bay stood against the pulling, suspicious of the odd behavior but willing to stand. The bay was a good one.

He settled in the saddle, wrapped the single rein around the horn, and wound his hands in the thick, coarse mane. Left alone, the bay would find his way home, to the Three V. To the old man. There was no other place for him to go.

The river had saved him, the icy-cold shock of the water, the cleansing numbness, even the peaceful moment just before the shotgun blast. The wounds were not serious; what he needed was rest and food. But what he had to do now was to ride on. He had enough to stop Duncan, and to put the word out on Fowler.

For his own death would go back to Duncan, reported by his killer. He knew for certain that it had been Hardin Fowler waiting for him. Joe managed a grim smile, then touched spur to the bay and hauled him with the one rein back onto the trail. It was a long ride ahead.

The pain became everything; the trotted miles, the weary stumbling as the bay got closer to the home ranch. Each step drove a spur into Joe's back. His hands wound deeper into the safety of the black mane. The bay traveled sideways at first, moving with the one rein tied to the horn, the other dangling free. He veered often from the trail, sometimes headed for a blade of grass, other times spooking from a darting shadow. Each time Joe drove the spurs in deeper, until the bay finally settled to the miles.

The bay headed for the back barn and walked through the carelessly opened door. Shod hooves rattled on the wood-plank floor and raised Joe in the saddle. That sound was a special sound in a land where most floors were dirt. He remembered laying the floor with his pa, and Hank, so careful to shove the boards tight into one another. The sound was unmistakable.

The horse stood still. Joe reached out to the wall and felt its support as he slid from the saddle and fell against a stall door. The flare of pain forced a grunt from clenched teeth. He took precious time to pull the bridle from the bay head and let it fall, to hang by one rein snugged to the horn. The bay trailed the bridle into an empty stall and began on a pile of sweet hay, oblivious of the dangling leather and metal.

The house. Being so close to his goal gave him renewed strength. He let go of the supporting door and took one step, and another. He would make it. Then a toe caught on a warped board and staggered him. He fought the gravity, spun halfway around and grabbed for the swinging stall door. It came back too fast and hit him knee-height. He went backward with the blow, and his head snapped as he hit the hard wooden floor. The bay continued working at the hay pile; inside the box stall a small cream-colored filly nickered with growing hunger. Joe was still, sprawled across the narrow aisle.

Chapter 16

Every evening, after the supper chores were done, they went to the old back barn and fed the small filly. It had become their time to sit deep in the straw and watch the antics of the uncertain foal. And talk. Lucy had been at the ranch for a week now, and the lines in her face were softening, the harshness easing. Elissa made her laugh, talking about her past and her travels. The sound of their laughter echoed in the once-empty barn.

This night Elissa pushed the heavy door back and let Lucy slip under her arm. In her other hand she had the warmed milk in a shallow tin bucket. The filly was learning to suck from the bucket and had started nuzzling at the sweet grain offered her. Elissa took one step

140

to follow and bumped into Lucy's back. Both women looked down at the loose body angled across the floor. Lucy raised the lantern to see the pale, thick hair and newly scarred face of Joe Gilead. A darkness of blood had spread from his back and stained the floor around him.

Lucy knelt to his head, and her strong fingers found the pulse at his jaw, slow and strong. She glanced at Elissa, at the wavering lantern in her hand, the moving light making uneven patterns in the shadowed barn.

Joe heard a thump as something landed by his head, felt the touch at his jaw. His eyes opened and shut rapidly from the yellow light too close. It took a moment for him to identify the noises and the smells that were so strange.

The rustling sound, soft, continuous, close by his ear; the smell of a hint of flowers, a cleanness out of place in a barn, around stock. Then he felt the touch again, this time on his forehead, lightly stroking the side of his face, pushing his hair from his eyes. A woman's touch. He opened his eyes again and began the struggle to sit. A strong hand guided him at the neck, supporting his efforts.

As he sat, one hand reached for the door, and he looked around. Very slowly. He could hear a quick intake of breath, a harsh sob, then the rustling noise ceased, and a face came in front of his. Lucy Fowler. A face he knew well. Joe smiled at the apparition and got a smile in return. He slowly brought up his other hand, almost lost his tenuous balance, and touched the face so

141

near his, felt the weathered skin under his fingers' search.

This was no ghost, but Lucy Fowler, sitting in the middle of a barn, on the floor, looking at him with a puzzled expression that flitted across her face. Pretty Lucy, sweet Lucy, who'd never had the time to talk with him, with the baby brother. Pretty Lucy who never knew he had loved her so. Joe smiled.

How could he grin at her? Blood covered his back, soaked into his pants, stained the floor where he had lain for lord knew how long. Yet here he sat, grinning as if there were nothing more serious than a game going on. There was something special about Joe Gilead.

"What happened to you, Joe? What brought you back here?" The question was reasonable, but Joe found the answer complicated.

"Got shot, sure enough, Lucy. You can see that. And went for a swim. Guess the bay brought me back here." He looked up beyond the kneeling woman and saw the tall form of Elissa. "Thank your pa for me, miss; that bay is a good one."

Lucy wanted to scold him for the answers, but he broke into her beginning tirade with more serious words.

"I know who heads the thieves, and how they get their information. Came back to tell my pa, then I can go. Paid him all I can. You ladies clean me up, make me presentable. Night's sleep and some food, and I can do my talking and be done."

He knew Lucy would ask for more, but he ducked his

142

head and shut his eyes, wanting to pretend exhaustion so she would not ask for names. The pretense was not needed; pain had returned to his back, building a pressure behind his eyes and covering his body with a fast-burning heat.

Lucy. He had to talk to Lucy. Joe looked up fast, and a whirling light-headedness turned him. Kneeling before him now was the lovely young woman who lived in his house. There was a danger in her closeness for him, and he tried to fight back, raising his hand to send her away, and letting go of the door.

The balance left him, and Joe toppled sideways, hitting the floor hard. He could hear a deep groan, a sound that must come from him. There was more warmth now, coming to his back and shoulders with the scraping of the barely scabbed holes. Hands shook him—he knew that—hands that rubbed the open sores, that kept him from sliding into the darkness.

For a short time Elissa could only kneel and watch the half-conscious man as he foundered weakly on his side, each move opening more holes to bleed freely. If he continued to fight, he would damage himself more, she could not wait for Lucy to return to help her. Elissa grabbed Joe by the shoulder, shook him hard, face close to his, fear for him overcoming her panic.

"Sit up; lean on me; help me. You've got to move; please help me." She tugged harder at him, hands turning sticky red with the effort. Pulling his arm only brought another deep groan. But she had him sitting up again, staring back at her with blank emerald eyes, too bright, too blank. The weakness frightened her, and the fright turned to anger.

"Damn you, Gilead. Don't give up. You've got to move, get into a stall, and lie down where there's room. Damn you, help me."

Disbelief replaced the anger in Elissa as Joe's flushed face, usually so somber, so remote, held the ghost of a smile that turned into a wide grin as she swore again. Her words were softer this time, almost hidden in the rapid breathing. "Damn you, Joe Gilead."

He took the challenge and once more pulled himself to his knees, this time using her arms as balance. He could feel the warmth under his hands and could see a wave of red flush across her face. Then she stood, pulling him up with her, leaning against his weight.

Joe lurched forward and up, hands tight around her arm. Close to her, close enough that it was natural to lean forward that much more and kiss those lovely lips, touch that mouth that offered so much. Joe let his body fall against her and held the kiss by inert force. She did not struggle under the kiss. They stayed together for a long time.

Lucy was motionless in the barn doorway for some of that time. Envy was her first reaction. And jealousy. She knew she was not seeing Hank, and she had no hold on this younger brother. But the stir of feelings was there, and she could only wait and watch.

"Joe." The word came softly to him, deep in a dream, surrounded by a clean warmth, a soft breath.

144

"Joe, we've got to treat your back." A hand came to touch him on the side of his face; he turned into the touch and saw Lucy's face close to his. A confusion of faces.

The two women steered the crumbling body backward into a stall. Sheer inertia brought him down, and then more hands rolled him onto his belly. A procession of pans, cloths, and a cobwebbed can holding a smelly concoction were put in a line near his eyes. Bits and pieces were picked up and put down.

The two women picked at the raw flesh. Bright moments of pain kept Joe awake, struggling not to curse or fight, mumbling into the straw bed. He could hear the soft voices above him, could feel the swift-moving hands. The women never flinched as they cleaned the bloody holes and covered them with the salve, but he could hear distress in a quick intake of breath, the smothered gasp, as a particular hole bled too freely and would not stop. He fought to stay conscious; there was a peculiar pleasure in the touch of the two women, a closeness he had missed for a long time. He lay in the straw, fighting to keep his body from jumping at the quick pain.

Lucy and Elissa worked as quickly as they could, knowing the pain they were causing, and wondering at the grim discipline of their patient, who endured so much in silence.

Chapter 17

"We need the doctor. It's more than I can handle. Elissa, you go get Mr. Travers." Lucy looked up from the prone man, hands red, dress front spotted, face streaked with sweat and dried blood. She smiled at the girl and tilted her head to the dark shape in a back stall. "Joe left your father's horse there. Take him."

Elissa nodded and backed the gelding out. The horse grunted with each step, and the heavy bit banged loudly on the end partition, startling both the horse and the two women. She led the horse out into the yard and let him drink sparingly, then walked along the corral lines, avoiding the long yellow streamers of light from the house. She finally mounted just beyond the reaching light, and urged the tired bay into a trot. Conflicting memories came with her as she went to the small cross-roads known as Resolution.

Illness was not new to Lucy. She had nursed her mother for the last year and had tended to injured hands on the Wagon Wheel. She looked Joe over carefully and shook her head. He would not stay down on the straw pallet; he would not give in to the fever but had struggled to sit up, carefully wedged in a corner of the stall, the triangular edge giving support without touching the grease-covered holes. The night had turned cold, and Lucy draped a blanket across his chest, tucking it in gently at each shoulder, bringing herself up against him as she so gently pushed and prodded. Fever brightened

146

the green eyes, but the remembered smile still came for her.

"Lucy, you 'member sneaking off to find Hank, 'sposed to be schooling? But we cut out, found him and Hardin wrestling down a yearling Pa told them to leave be." The words were slurred and came in uneven bursts, but she remembered the day. She was twelve, Joe not yet ten, and Hardin and Hank a lofty seventeen, too old to continue school. Her figure was beginning to push out her dresses, and when she saw Hank Gilead, a funny feeling came over her.

"I 'member you putting a bandage on me then, tore hell out of my arm coming out that shed door. Made me hold still for your doctoring, hurt like hell. You 'ways liked to care for folks, girl. Still doing it.

"A grown woman now and still looking to take care of folks. A good woman. Remember that, Lucy." His voice faded, and his head slumped for a moment on his chest. Lucy marveled at the drive in Joe that kept him sitting beside her, that had held him to the saddle for the long ride back home. This was a man she could have loved. And then she remembered the two of them, young Elissa and this man, bodies locked together. Elissa's eyes had come to her over Joe's shoulder, wide in wonderment and pleasure. Joe Gilead was spoken for.

"Lucy, got to tell Pa. Got to tell him the man. Tomorrow morning, get me put together, and I'll tell Pa. Don't want him knowing 'bout being shot. Just want to tell him and ride."

147

He could see the distress rise in Lucy's face and slowly put out a hand for comfort. "I can ride, Lucy. Been hurt worse than this and ridden on. Just get me presentable for Pa." He tried a smile, then touched the end of her nose and rubbed quickly, drawing a small smile in return.

Lucy jerked awake from a slight noise. An anxious voice close to her called her name, and she awoke to padding feet on the bare floor. Elissa was at the stall door; behind her came the shadowed figure of the doctor, heavy leather bag in hand.

"Asleep? Good. Miss Elissa told me everything." The girl moved aside to let the portly doctor inside. He was on his knees before reaching Joe, and his skilled hands ran over the injured man's face, pulled up one eyelid, felt for the pulse. Both eyes came open, and Joe grinned innocently at the round face before him.

It took another hour to find and remove the remaining black pellets from Joe's back and upper arms. Some of the shot were deeply embedded, demanding a sharp probe and repeated applications of alcohol to clear the bleeding. Others had traveled just under the skin and came out with a gentle pinching.

Travers had no chloroform, so he put his mouth to Joe's ear and told him. There could be no shouting, no noise that would draw the old man to the barn. Joe knew and tried to mouth the words but failed. The operation went on in grim silence until the doctor came to one bunching of pellets along his side. Joe arched under

148

the searching knife and went limp. Travers checked—
pulse strong, breathing steady—so he continued the
crude operation.

It was past four in the morning, the sky beginning to
streak with lighter hints, when the doctor left the small
barn, hurrying to the patient horse tied in the brush.
Lucy went to the house to be ready and waiting as the
ranch crew woke for the day. Lucy would deal with the
ordinary morning chores, then Elissa would come in to
get the old man.

So Elissa sat and watched the sleeping man. She
knew she should be tired, but a nervous edge kept her
eyes open, her heart racing erratically. The patient slept
comfortably now, the fever burned from him during the
long night, face pale, buried sideways in the yellow
straw as he lay on his belly.

A despair invaded her tiredness. It had been Lucy's
hands that steadied the twitching flesh, that plucked the
slippery shot from exposed flesh, Lucy's words that
soothed the rise of fever, Lucy's calm humor that held
her through the night. She felt tears come to her eyes,
burn her flesh, but not ease the pain inside her. She had
come to a crisis and had failed.

"Miss, it's over. All over now. I thank you for your
help." The quiet voice brought her back from her fears,
and she watched once again as the wounded man struggled to rise from the pallet.

"Need to see Pa, need a clean shirt, need . . ." His
voice faded, and she felt the pity well inside her, then

had to stifle a giggle at his next words.

"A good-sized steak, biscuits, and a quart of coffee. At least a quart. That's what I need. Then Pa. You sure look like a candidate for breakfast." Joe smiled back at the laughter she was strangling. "You think hunger's funny, miss. I got a hunger that only half a beef can cure. Bet you could handle a good-sized bite yourself."

Joe caught the infection and joined it, letting the relief of laughter erase the night. He was hungry, and ready to talk, ready to release his obligation and ride on. Instinct made him crave secrecy; Duncan thought him dead, and Hardin was the murderer. He had come up one last time in the icy waters, and he thought but was not certain that a hand had come up from the figure on the bank and had saluted him as he went under one more time. The figure was Hardin Fowler.

The quick shift from light teasing to harsh scowl went across Joe's face, and Elissa read the change. She sobered quickly, and in the silence stood and left the small barn to walk to the warm invitation of the ranch house. Inside was the old man, waiting for the morning to begin. Now, before too many were about, was the time for the old man to see his son. A quick trip through the kitchen to stuff a few biscuits in her apron pocket, and Elissa found the old man in the big rocker by the south window, staring out to watch the mist rising with the sun's growing strength. He looked up at her approach; a steaming cup sat near his elbow, and a plate with more of those biscuits was on the floor by his boot. She smiled. Finally there was something good she could bring to this kind old man.

"Mr. Evan, Joe's in the back barn. He's waiting for you. He's been hurt, but we had the doctor with him last night, and he'll be fine. Just tired now, and sore. He wants to see you. He said best to keep quiet around my father."

Her pleasure grew as she watched the seamed face open to a smile, the faded eyes lighten. He did not question her but stood slowly, carefully, one hand searching for the cane. Nor did he ask why she picked up the full cup, careful not to spill the warm coffee. He only nodded good morning to her father as they passed him, face dark with the day's concerns. John Stratmeyer barely noticed them as they passed and did not return the greeting.

"Joe." The old man stood at the stall door and looked down at his son. Elissa knelt to the young man and handed him another shirt, wincing with him as the soft material found the open sores. The father said nothing, only watched the young woman care for his son. A brief glint came and went in the old eyes, too quick to be seen. He leaned on the heavy cane and sighed deeply.

"I know who the rustler is, and the traitor. It's Ed Duncan leading them, and Hardin Fowler's his man. Hardin shot me; Duncan set me up good."

The facts stood wide open in the silence. The two men watched each other, and Elissa knew she was an intruder. Yet she was unwilling to leave.

"Fowler came in midmorning yesterday, had a long talk with Duncan. Took more of your cattle. Duncan

151

had me ride along with him." A deep bitterness crept into the factual tone. "We did some wild riding, took Duncan and his men through the badlands, out beyond Resolution. Found that old trail to Blackman's." Joe watched his father's face, waiting for the disapproval. There was nothing to be seen.

"Must of been a real pleasure for Duncan to let Hardin take his shot. Sent me on a fool's errand, and Hardin was waiting. Duncan thinks he's home free now. He'll take all he can and ride out, and I'm betting he plans to leave Hardin behind a dead man. He sure got something on his mind."

Evan knew what Duncan was planning. Hardin had sat in his corner two nights past, listening, saying nothing, taking a quick drink from a tin flask. Fowler knew all about the big gather, so Duncan knew the big plans that were going to protect the ranchers. The big man must be laughing at his own joke.

"Joe, we got a big idea to join together, all the ranches hereabouts, have one big roundup. And we plan to hold the stock in Blackman. Duncan must be loving how we fell right into his hands."

There was a silence between the two men. Joe leaned back against the wall and winced as flesh touched hard board. The discomfort kept his mind working. Then the old man almost spoke, but Joe's words came first, in a labored stream following his thoughts.

"Give me picked men, good men, and I can set an ambush the backside of Blackman's. Before the gather's complete. You set men to guard the entrance;

tell no one what we're doing. Just get me ten, twelve, good men who'll fight hard. We can take Duncan easily and end this forever."

"Boy, you ain't in no shape to ride, never mind fight."

"There's time now. Duncan's greed will want as many beefs as possible. Give me time to heal."

Joe did not want the concern he saw in the lined face. He wanted only to discuss plans, set a time, deal with the threat. He shut his eyes and dropped his head, hoping the signs would be read. There was nothing for a while, then a tapping that interrupted heavy steps, that became fainter. The old man was gone. Joe opened his eyes to find the girl still there. Her mouth opened as if to spit out the anger showing in her eyes, but he averted his face and rolled gently back down into the deep straw bedding. Her softer footsteps followed the old man's, and then he was alone.

Chapter 18

The visit to Wagon Wheel left John Stratmeyer restless, and more worried. Fowler was drunk, not even midmorning, and the man was sodden-stinking drunk. He had nothing but complaints; Lucy's desertion, the lack of graze. John knew more about Fowler's married life than he had any right to. What he knew was meant to stay between husband and wife. He couldn't wait to leave.

His patience was planed to nonexistence as he led the wet chestnut into the pen. In the back of his mind he cursed again the thief who'd stolen his good bay. He stripped the chestnut and loosed it in the corral with absent moves, then stopped and took another look at the penned horses. The crooked blaze, the high black stockings, the compact body. Thinner now, the gloss dulled, ribs showing, burrs matting the thick tail, but he would know that horse anywhere.

He barely saw Lucy and did not notice the dark circles at her eyes or the tiredness to her walk. A quick search of the kitchen found his daughter stirring something at the blackened range.

"Girl, Shook's back. How? Did the law return him?" A growing conviction took hold. "That damned son is here, isn't he? You two are hiding him. It's not the foal that's sick: you two're nursing an outlaw out in that back barn. Right under my roof."

Lucy spoke before Elissa, wanting the words to come from her, hoping to protect the girl from her own father's anger.

"Mr. Stratmeyer, Joe's home. And wounded. And yes, he's in the back barn. His father's been out there; they've talked. Tonight he'll come to the house to stay. Mr. Evan asked for you to come talk with him before you do anything. Says it's real important." Her voice rose without her usual control. "Don't you yell at that old man; it's still his ranch. And his son."

The truth in her words stopped Stratmeyer. His mind flicked back to the bay horse in the corral, the horse thief in the barn, and the old man waiting for him, most likely in the small office. He turned on his heel and ignored his daughter, refusing to see the distress in her flushed face, the anger draining Lucy's complexion. He would talk to the old man now.

Evan Gilead met him at the door. His face warned Stratmeyer to go gently. "You listen. My boy is back, and your horse is returned. So forget the itch under your saddle and listen to me." Pushed none too gently by the determined old man, Stratmeyer sat in front of the cluttered desk and kept his temper.

"Joe rode with them rustlers, John. Did it deliberate-like. Knows the boss now. Ed Duncan. Bet that one sticks in your gut. Was with them thieves that took the last herd. Taking your horse was Joe's ticket in. Now we got us some planning to do, so you listen and let go of that bite of vengeance that's poking at you."

Stratmeyer listened and forgot his bitter contempt. Here were names and facts he could deal with, ideas that made sense. Together they worked on a list of men Joe could trust, who would accept his word and his leadership. John settled into the hard oak chair and shrugged off the heavy jacket. He and the old man became equals in the fight ahead.

Hardin Fowler didn't hear the two horses in the corral. He hadn't been outside yet that day, and the horses nickered their hunger each time his shape crossed a window. But he did not hear their invitation or see the empty hay rick and dry water tank. For Hardin Fowler was drunk again. Had been drunk since he'd ridden in four days ago and put up the shotgun without cleaning it. That day he'd remembered to feed the stock and send the small crew out to check for imaginary losses on cut fence.

They would be back today or had come and gone yesterday. Two men, who feared losing even this poor job, riding for a drunken boss. Hardin pulled himself up against the door frame and turned his back on the outdoors. There were bottles standing upright, lying on their side, some with an inch of amber liquor showing. The main room was littered with the bottles, and the kitchen wall had a dusty black spot above the range, the remnants of a bacon fire Hardin had put out with a dose of whiskey.

He snorted. Food be damned. Where was another bottle? Back in his memory he could hear John Stratmeyer's voice, droning on about some kind of plan. Plans. Damned fool man and his plans. Stratmeyer had ridden in just after Joe Gilead's death. Now there were two dead Gileads to haunt him. He found the bottle and tipped it back against his eager lips.

Hardin became frantic; the bottle was near-empty, and he knew there was no more whiskey in this place. Then he steadied himself and grinned owlishly. Two more weeks, or maybe three, and he could buy all the whiskey he wanted, could send a "man" into town if 'n he didn't want to make the trip himself.

To hell with his wife; to hell with her pa and all the stuffy bastards who ran this end of the Dakotas. In two weeks time he would have them in his back pocket. He coughed and bent double, then wiped his chin with his fingers and rattled the empty glass bottle. That last inch tasted good, and Hardin made a wandering path through the house, picking up each bottle and drawing the last bit of liquor from it. Two more weeks.

There were some words he remembered from the thin rancher's visit. A date. A number. A huge number beyond his expectations. The canyon. Goddamn it, Blackman's canyon. Seems old Evan had set that one up. Only one entrance, easy to guard.

Yet Duncan said Blackman was no problem. Laughed at Hardin's worries and told him Joe Gilead had given them Blackman's. Then Stratmeyer came at him again, demanding riders, horses, supplies, all for this fool effort. So that's where the two riders must have gone. Probably took his whiskey with them. The fools. Duncan and he were too smart for them. The fools.

A face came to him as he slumped in the chair. A smiling face, eyes wide-spaced and brown, thick, dark hair falling across the laughter. Or were they green eyes, full of suspicion and distrust, set in the same wide face?

Hardin lifted a hand from the last bottle and swiped at the apparition weaving in front of him. A name came with the ghost: Hank. But that weren't right. Hank didn't have those blazing green eyes; Hank's were a dull hazel brown, banished now beneath the years of dirt. Hank didn't have a back full of buckshot; Hank had no head, the skull showing white through the bloody featureless pulp. Why did Hank keep coming to him?

Hardin screamed at the face blurring in front of him and stood up to fight. The face slipped backward, away from him, taunting him with slippery features.

He lunged at the face, struck out at the engaging Gilead smile. Falling through the empty space, Hardin came up against the scarred desk and rolled heavily to the floor. Dead drunk and worn out fighting his murdered ghosts.

Chapter 19

Lucy was sick every morning. The old man stayed away from her and away from the room that held his son. This time Elissa was glad to tend to the injured Joe Gilead. He had come to the house after midnight, moving cautiously so that none of the men saw his long, slow walk between Elissa and her reluctant father. He must remain dead or banished to the rest of the basin.

The injured man lay on his belly, head propped sideways in the soft down pillows. Yesterday he smiled at her, tried for a feeble joke that drew a quick giggle from her and a slow smile from him. She never would have thought this man could smile.

In that short time the puckered holes were healing. The doctor had been out, ostensibly for Lucy's care, and when he learned the particulars of Joe's ride in the Little Missouri, told him it probably was the most life-giving bath he would ever have.

"Washed that damned infection right out of you; froze

158

to death anything figuring to make you sick. Wouldn't suggest that particular method to most folks, but it seems to have been successful with you." Travers laughed at his nonsense and was startled at the responding grin from Joe.

Elissa watched the transformation and could not forget past words. Rested, comfortable in the familiar bed, the face showed its handsomeness the mother had once talked about. The smile brought kind wrinkles to his eyes, softened the harsh set to his mouth, and somehow erased the network of old and new scars that had taken his youth.

This morning she had a special treat for Joe, fresh hot bread and wild plum preserves found in the almost-empty cellar under the old kitchen. She could not wait to see his enjoyment.

The tray almost tipped its burden when Elissa came into the room and found the bed empty, covers thrown back in a tumbled mass. But she steadied herself and righted the tray, forcing a smile when she found him standing at the window, watching the yard empty of riders as her father gave out the day's work.

"They don't know I'm here; no one knows I'm here. Right?" Joe did not turn from the window nor make any attempt to know who had entered the room. He waited for the answer.

"No. No one 'cepting your father, and mine. Lucy, and the doctor, too. The rest think you're riding with the rustlers. Utah saw to that. No one else knows you're alive, and you won't stay that way if you get up and

159

move around too soon." Concern harshened her manner, bringing Joe's head around from the window.

Pleasure flooded through him as he looked at the young woman standing near the small table, hands on her hips, ordering him back to bed. The fine blond hair had already escaped its morning pinning, and the light cotton dress she wore flowed over her body like fine silk. Joe recognized his feelings. He had glimpsed them briefly before. They had twisted into him when he watched the funeral, and the doctor, his hand touching her arm.

Love. Not just the reflex to bed a desirable woman, but a love that could go on over the years. He had given up all chance for decent love when he'd smashed his brother's face, but he could not drive down the tenderness that overwhelmed him when this certain young woman touched him, changed his bandages, or tended to his basic needs.

Something of his thought must have shown on his face. The past few days had dulled his hard-earned instinct for survival, his ability to mask his feelings. In this quiet and friendly room, that most essential ability had left him, and now he stood exposed in front of the enemy. For her kindness and beauty were thieves that would rob him of his life.

Elissa could read this face now, and what she saw made her drop her fists and walk slowly to the man by the window. Her hands came up to touch his chest as she stood near him. A look foreign to Joe softened her already-beautiful face, lowered her eyelids, and lent a

160

heaviness to her parted lips. He had seen the look mimicked by countless women, those looking for money for their favors. But here, in front of him, touching him so gently on bandaged chest, was this young woman offering her desire.

He was powerless. Her mouth found his, and he answered the light pressure with a more demanding force. They stepped no closer to each other, stayed united only by their lips and the light embrace of her hands. For a short moment Joe could forget everything: the past deaths, the present wounds, the future battle.

With a vicious twist of his head he backed away from the lightly swaying girl. His brother's face had come to float between them.

"Miss, you get out now. I don't need no more nursing. You don't want to remember, do you? You don't want doings with a murderer, and I'm a killer. That's no life for you."

He turned back to the window, the clear glass reflecting his own drawn face and the tears welling down the cheeks of the woman motionless behind him. He could see it all, could watch her hands rise in a helpless gesture to her mouth as if to find an answer. Then the fine head dropped, and she walked away from him, past the still-steaming coffee and the small pile of bread and jam on the table. Joe watched from the glass window until he could no longer see her, then he limped to the bed, where he sat heavily and stared at the now-bitter meal. He was right, but the pain was unbearable.

He did not know how long he'd been sitting there.

The coffee was cold, the soft slices of bread already curling in the dry air, when his father's cane prodded the door fully open, and the old man shuffled his way inside.

"What'd you do to that girl? She's been your nurse and your protector, boy. What'd you do to her to leave her crying. It was wrong, boy, whatever you did."

"There's nothing to us, old man, and it's none of your business. When this rustling's settled, I'm gone. And I can't see asking her to ride with me."

His father's voice held the same roughness. "I've learned the forgiveness, boy. Now you got to learn the same. And you got to live, not just survive. You surely ain't got much of a life now."

The words should have hurt, but he had grown up under this man and knew him well. The kindness was real, the forgiveness genuine, and the blunt words a cover to his goodness. There was no subterfuge in the rancher, only a forthright honesty that could not be dulled. Joe knew the love was there, but when he looked into the tired face he saw Hank. He could not live with that face every day. Battling the image at night was enough.

He also knew that to talk would bring out better arguments than he could counter. So he turned away from the emotions and to the practical. "I'm ready to ride now. Sooner'n the doc thought. Need to do some riding, get in shape. I'll go at night; be needing a real quiet horse. Don't want any of the hands seeing me. Be needing more clothes, too. Nothing new, can't be buying anything that would make anyone wonder. You see to all this, and I'll start tonight."

He would keep talking until the temptation to cradle the old man's words to his heart would leave him. Words would push the old man away, would let him keep his pain private and buried deep inside. He could focus on the immediacy of the fight. The action of the battle would be good. Tonight he would ride.

Chapter 20

Ed Duncan was a big man, not in his height but in the breadth of his back and the width of his ambitions. He could only laugh at the haggard face of Hardin Fowler, who stood before him, leaning against his lathered sorrel, worry fighting for space with the red lines of drink on the man's face.

"There's going to be too many for us, Duncan. Too many ranchers, too many cowhands, too goddamn many beefs for us to move. We got to refigure, got to think of something . . ."

Hardin Fowler was purely a coward, a small man living inside a bottle, who one day would not come out. Duncan shoved aside the unsteady figure and turned his back to walk into the cabin. His mind checked all the possibilities; he had it all figured: that number, the magic number of ten thousand head, give or take a few thousand. And he planned to take more than just a few thousand. The word was out—he needed more men. And he'd been looking for buyers. Les Bristol down on the plains, he'd take three thousand easy. And Blake Wooster over to the Montana side, he'd move another four. There were other men, sharing his greed, who would pay cash, vent the brands, and move the herds another county or state away. Ten thousand wasn't anything to fret about.

Ed felt a hand grab at his shoulder, and he spun around, striking at the intruder without bothering to know the name. Fowler's head flew back from the blow, and the man backpedaled, slipping on the softly yielding pine needles. Duncan stood over the fallen man, legs wide, hands clenching and loosening in a vicious rhythm. He was getting crazy spending all his time out here. He stepped over Fowler, not bothering to see the hand coming up, asking for help.

He wanted a look at Elissa Stratmeyer, another look, maybe even a touch. He hitched his pants up over his sliding belly and shook his head. There was a growing restlessness to him that the bar girls did nothing to appease. Women surely messed up a man's thoughts. He needed to be clearheaded for the coming raid. Holding a group of thieves and murderers in the small canyon was tapping his energies.

But he couldn't keep his mind from the tall girl with the long blond hair and regal walk. When she had looked at him that last time, there was only disgust in her face, and pity for the beaten man at his feet. But he had seen the willowy body, the fine hair, slender hands that could drive a man wild. He refused to keep the memory of the fear and disgust rising in her eyes.

Just perhaps, after the Three V folded under its losses, and her pa saw his life disappear in the dust of the stolen herd, then just perhaps she would see him as he was, would listen to his proposal, coming as it would from a cleaned-up and wealthy Edwin Duncan, riding a big, spotted studhorse and doffing a pearl-gray Stetson custom-made just for him. Perhaps.

Fool. Thoughts like that only rob a man. Take his common sense and let him think with his crotch. But Duncan felt the thinking stay with him, linger in his mind as he sat and waited for the slow arrival of his small army. He needed action.

"Carson, I'm going out. Need to check in Resolution, buy me some more cigars. Maybe a few other pretties that fit in the saddlebag."

The smaller man shook his head, not bothering to answer the boss. Instinct told him the words weren't for him but to soothe something itching at the boss. He could wait another few days, or a week. Duncan mounted the sturdy gray and put him to a lope, taking them both out of the shrinking confines of the canyon.

The ride to Resolution had been a sham; he'd bought cigars and had a drink in the almost-empty bar just to satisfy his words back at the canyon. Carson didn't care, but Duncan went through the motions, killing time until he could ride past the Three V in the dark. Questions aimed at the barkeep brought only surly grunts. And few answers. Most of the drinkers had been hired up, out on some damn fool roundup that was going to end all the troubles round here. Well, said the barkeep, his troubles were growing with the hiring of each man. Soon enough the bar would close, probably find him out there chasing them beefs along with his customers. Some solution to the troubles in the Resolution basin.

Duncan snorted at the drivel, and let the man wander on with his talk. Sure was going to end the troubles. All them ranchers would be wiped out and dead broke, if not downright dead. And he, Edwin Duncan, would be the richer.

The gray wasn't in any more hurry than the rider when their path crossed the end of the long valley belonging to the Gileads. Duncan knew the path well. Down at its end was the old man, alone with his buried wife and sons, and the water-soaked corpse he didn't know about. But right now, that Gilead had something in his house belonging to Duncan. A young filly just waiting for the right stud to court her.

He swung the gray around without thinking and put the horse to the once-familiar path, then hauled the gray in hard. He could make out the shape of a horse and rider coming toward him, moving at a slow walk, deliberate and even-paced. There was enough light and shadow for him to know it was a woman riding toward him.

For three nights in a row Joe had saddled up and ridden out on a pensioned-off bay. His father said nothing but watched his son struggle with the heavy gear and finally swing it over the sagging back. Elissa fussed, threatened to ride with him as a baby-sitter. The savagery in Joe's refusal frightened her, startled the old man, and made her take two steps back. She stood by the father and watched the son battle to pull himself onto the patient horse.

But he could not stop her from following him. The first night Joe barely got to the end of the canyon walls, keeping the old horse to a willing walk, making it easy for her to follow. She sighed with relief as he turned the bay toward the big house and was thankful he knew there were some limits to his strength. He rode slumped over, both hands on the shiny worn leather of the swell, rocking with each ponderous step that the horse took.

The next night he'd ridden farther, putting the bay to a slow jog, gone for almost an hour and coming back to the barn soaked in sweat and eyes bright with exhaustion. But the success pushed him on, and tonight he had put the bay to a slow lope almost immediately and was gone beyond the limits of the high-walled valley. Once outside she had lost him. Elissa kept her mare to a walk, searching in the thin dark light for some sign of the horse and rider. She did not see the heavyset man on the big gray until they stepped out from the shadowed rock. But her mare jerked to a stop and threw up her head at the clumsy hand clamped on her bridle.

"Well, missy, out for a moonlight ride. And in the darkness. How nice and sweet. Perhaps you figured on meeting your intended. Well, missy, here I am, ready and waiting for you."

The ill-defined face did not show to Elissa, but the

biting, insinuating voice brought a shiver to her back. Ed Duncan. The ex-brawler, the ugly-eyed man who would stare at her until she broke down and looked away. The one who would stay to watch her mount a horse, making that brief moment when her leg showed as she swung over the saddle become an indecency.

She shuddered at the thickness to Duncan's voice but held her silence, mindful that Joe Gilead was out there ahead of her, perhaps even now riding back toward the house, back to an unexpected meeting with his enemy. For she knew what such a meeting would bring: a violent and brutal fight with almost certain death for Joe. She shied away from the possibility.

She forced a smile to encourage the man. In the dark Duncan might not be able to see her face, but the smile helped her prepare the words. She must put all her talent into believing what she was about to say.

"Ed, you did surprise me. I've missed you on the ranch, but I'm expected back at the house, or we could stay and . . . talk." The pause had to be timed just right, the catch in her voice an unsaid invitation. The slowness of the next words pulled the man even deeper. "Perhaps we could meet another time?"

For all his size and brains, Duncan could be a fool like any man. And he became a fool listening to the sweet unsaid words from the beautiful Elissa. That voice offered to him, created an anticipation in him that would drive him crazy. He kneed the gray to stand broadside with the mare and reached over to pull Elissa partway from the saddle. He found her mouth in the darkness and separated her lips with a force that drove her teeth into her lower lip. He could taste the blood and yet she did not cry out or struggle.

Over Duncan's shoulder, Elissa could see a black horseman silhouetted against the lightness of the sand wall disappear down the Three V trail. For a moment longer she accepted the brutal kiss, until the shadowed horseman was gone, then struggled against the pull, kicking the mare, digging her spur into soft flesh, making the mare shift angrily into the gray.

Duncan knew he'd gone far enough, for now. Further than he had thought possible. But the filly was willing. It did not enter his overcharged mind that she had become willing only for a short instant, that she had never shown such interest in the past. That her reaction had always been one of disgust. The nights of imaging her underneath him in the blankets had warped his reality. He wanted to believe she had missed him, and so he accepted the whispered pleadings and let her go. He watched the dark mare walk on beyond his vision, then stabbed the gray painfully and whirled up the steeply angled trail, unmindful of the noise.

Joe heard the sounds of a fast-moving horse and pulled in the bay. He waited, hearing the hoofbeats fade; then there was only silence. Finally another horse could be heard, coming slowly toward him. He backed the bay up against the wall and waited. As the rider came in front of him, he nudged the bay a step forward, blocking the trail.

It took only the quick intake of breath for him to

know the rider. But her presence did not explain the other sounds, of a horse going away from the ranch trail. Joe loosened his reins, and the bay stood comfortably, touched the mare's nuzzle, then sighed, and rubbed gently along the soft neck. These two horses were old friends.

"Who was riding with you, girl? I told you to leave me be."

Fear and a lingering disgust robbed her of a careful answer.

"Why, damn you, Joe Gilead, you don't own me. I can ride where I please and anytime I please. Who I meet is my business. Now let me pass." Her voice shook on the last words as she yanked at the quiet mare.

She raised her face to stare at him, and there was enough light for her to see Joe, to read the pain on his face, and something else she could not name. She wanted to touch him, to soothe away the buried anger, but the snorting mare saved her from another mistake. She spun the mare into a run, headed for the small comfort of the ranch.

Joe started the bay gelding after the girl, but the labored strides of the tired old horse and the corresponding twinge across his back soon made him rein in the horse and settle to a walk. For anything would involve him closer with her, and he could not be near her and not want her. Near enough to her to breathe in her scent, to see the soft texture of her skin, the count of fine long hairs that daily escaped their confinement. As long as he kept his distance he was safe.

Daylight became a torture for Joe; restlessness drove him to walk in circles in the small room upstairs. Sleeping during the heat of the day, riding for longer periods each night, he healed fast. By wordless agreement he did not see the girl, and she managed to leave his meals and pick up after him while he was riding. She no longer followed behind him. The only human contact he had now was the few visits from Edgar Travers, and Joe deliberately passed by the words put out in gesture of friendship. He would leave no bonds in this house. A few more days and he would be gone for good.

But the restlessness drove him out early one morning, unable to settle on the bed and sleep. He walked carefully into the long, dark main room, listening intently. There were few sounds echoing in the big house. Upstairs he knew in which room Elissa slept—across from her father's room, in what had been his mother's sewing room. The main bedroom downstairs usually echoed the grunts and wheezes signaling the interrupted sleep of the old man. Joe hesitated; this morning he could hear nothing.

"Waiting here for you, boy. Been hearing you come out here the past few mornings, figured this was a time I'd get here afore you, talk with you. Come set with me, boy. We got some things to settle out."

Caught. Waves raised soft hair on Joe's forearms, stiffened the bristly cut hair at the back of his neck. A gust of feeling close to panic shook him, weakened him at the knees. He could only walk slowly across the bare-plank floor, stockinged feet making no sound. The old man was waiting in the false dawn light.

There was a chair carefully positioned next to the big hard-backed old rocker that was the old man's favorite. Faint light let Joe see the outlines of the wrinkled face. "You can't run forever, boy. I know you have it in your mind to get once this is settled, that you see all this as a penance you have to pay. Just want you to know, boy, you can stay here forever. The past is gone, buried up on that cursed hill. The future is here for you, if you want it."

Generous words, but Joe had used that generosity too long and too cruelly. "Old man, let it go, let me go. Talk to me about the gather, but leave the rest. It can never be made right. I got to live with it every day."

There was a long silence. Each man sat with his own thoughts and searched for the escape. Finally the old man broke the stillness.

He went over the plans, the growth of the herd, the bait of the few guards at the entrance, the bluster of bringing in Hardesty as the law. Then he turned to Hardin Fowler, and the disgust in the old voice made the feelings easily read.

"The word keeps coming in Fowler is most always drunk, too damn drunk to work. Wouldn't of thought he had enough conscience to bother him. In 'nother day we can send him home. Tell him we're sorry he's poorly and send him out. Then we'll bring up your troop. I got Track running the show, picking the men.

172

He trusts you, boy, believes in you most as much as me. Near to broke his heart when he had to tell me he'd seen you riding that day. A good man, Track. Loyal as hell. Something I'm putting a high value on now.

"Soon as we send Fowler home, Duncan'll know the size of the herd. Them cattle will draw that man like sweet honey. You pick the spot, Track's got the men. I'll tell him tomorrow."

"The law will have something to say about all this, after we're done." Joe was surprised at his own words and doubly surprised at his father's grin.

"Already got that one figured out, too. Going to send out a relay of men once you in place. Over to Medora, to Hardesty. Tell the men to ride slow. Son of a bitch ain't too smart, but he'll truly appreciate getting a bunch of proven rustlers handed to him, dead or alive. Elections coming this fall, and he'll like being a hero."

Joe stood up from the chair and moved away from the confines of the comfortable setting. True dawn began to show its colors, and he could hear the triangle iron ringing, drawing sleeping men awake for their coffee, flapjacks, and steak. John Stratmeyer, and his daughter, would be coming down the stairs soon. Lucy would be sitting up, hair disheveled, wishing she could sleep a bit longer.

He came back to his father, wanting to say something to the old man, to thank him somehow for his faith. But the words froze. Light steps brought the young woman to stand at the top of the wide stairway, hands clasped

173

at the top of her flannel robe, eyes widened by the sight of him.

Joe flinched and drew back. He could not allow her in his thoughts. The smell of the hot coffee came to him; the clean, sleepy face above him promised so much; the twisted figure settled in the worn chair offered a place. Panic put Joe moving fast for the safety of the small room, then froze him as he realized he had to pass the girl. He looked up again, and she had disappeared; he turned his head, and his father was staring out the window. He was almost running when he finally found the half-open door and disappeared inside in safety.

Chapter 21

Anticipation tied a hard knot under Joe's belt. His hands trembled slightly as he tugged the cinch tighter on the black gelding. Briefly he cursed the good blue left back in the hidden canyon, but the black would do for the night's ride and the day's work.

The worst of the waiting was over—three weeks camping all day inside the big house. The walls had grown closer each day, and the dark rides were all that kept his sanity. Now he would ride in the bright daytime, and Track Williams would ride with him, with ten other men carefully chosen for their nerve and their abilities.

Track was nearby, his long frame leaning against the sullen blownup belly of his dun. A knee firmly planted in the expanded girth drove the extra air out, and Track

174

pulled the cinch up another three holes. Wouldn't do to have a saddle turn on him this ride. He glanced over at the once-familiar length of Joe Gilead. A slight stiffness to his movements was all that was left of the back of buckshot he'd taken over a month ago. Track winced as he thought of the long story the old man had told him. A real beaut, with more twists than Joe's cold ride down the Little Missouri.

Relief had been Track's first reaction, then a confusion of anger and pity. The old man would not look at him as he continued the tale. Now they would ride out, stake a spot on the ambush trail, and do some more waiting that would end in death for more than one man. These men riding with him, they knew their odds; none of them rode blind, and' all were eager to get moving.

Joe led the single file of riders, and Track brought up the rear, leading a reluctant pair of saddle horses as pack animals. Their burden was light in food and gear, and heavy with shells. Enough for each man to form his own branch of the cavalry. Only Joe knew exactly where the line of men was headed, and it had taken some fancy persuading from the old man before some of the riders would follow blindly behind this son of his. Joe they didn't know, and didn't trust, but the old man had their loyalty.

Utah Smith had been the toughest; by god he'd seen Joe Gilead riding with the damned thieves, and now he was being asked to surrender what he saw, what he knew about a real-enough thief, and follow his orders. Utah had a lot to say, and most of it not fit for human company. Track kept at him, wanting Utah beside him.

As usual, appealing to Utah's full-fledged vanity drew the trick out of the hat. Facts were fine, but what the eye took in wasn't always what it really saw. And being told you were sure enough a fancy shot and needed by the rest of these poor critters made a man swell up with a pride most agreeable and be willing to do anything. Track Williams knew his man. No one said Utah was bright, just a damned good shot.

Track grinned in the rising dust and jerked again on the line. The zebra-striped buckskin packing dinner snorted and put out a few strides of trot in return, then settled back into a quick and sullen walk. That one wasn't going to accept his demotion to pack mule with any grace at all. Track winked at the animal and spat a stream of tobacco into the print of the horse ahead of him. The ride was going to be long and grim.

Beyond the Three V valley and lined out just below the ridge, Joe put the black to a long trot, careful on the hard rock ground he chose to cross, ground that chipped at the horses' hooves but gave off little telltale dust. The line followed him, each man silently admiring the choice of trail. Perhaps the hard-faced rider on the sweat-streaked black would do to ride with.

Jack Allen glanced back quickly at his bunkmate. Wall Blaisdell caught the jerky movement and dropped his head once. Jack looked to the trail head. Good to know that Wall agreed. The next few days were looking to be something to remember.

176

Joe stopped more often now, jamming the men behind him with no warning, testing the tempers of their horses. He had to be certain of the trail. They were in deep scrub now, and off to one side they could see a thinning in the dense undergrowth that told of another, easier trail. Each time Gilead skirted an inviting clearing, careful to leave no signs of their movement, the men knew that sometime in the next day or two Ed Duncan would be riding with his murdering crew along that inviting line, straight through the clearings, headed right into a trap.

Bent grasses, broken twigs, fresh lines of horse droppings, would be a first-grade primer to the men riding with Duncan, so the riders struggled through the thick brush, hacking at limbs catching their clothing, scratching at face and hands. No one could see why, no one saw the reason to stop, but Joe's hand finally waved the line to halt. These men only knew the inviting mouth to Blackman's canyon, open, easy, with game trails leading in and out in a shallow maze. This confusion of brush and rocky ground was unknown to them. They could not see the rim of the canyon ahead of them and had to take their trail boss's word. They had no time to argue.

The spartan camp went up fast—a rope line between two stunted bushes to hold the stock. No cook fire, no need for firewood. Water, stale from its long ride against hot flesh, hard bread, beef jerky, airtights of tomatoes and peaches. A blanket for each man, a canteen of water, and a nosebag of oats for the horses. Thin rations, but the men knew the waiting would end soon, and this knowing silenced the usual grumbling.

Out of plain malice Duncan saddled the blue gelding. The hind shoe had been pulled and replaced, and the horse had grown sassy on the good grass and no work. Ed figured Joe Gilead wouldn't care now if the roan turned outlaw. He grinned at the righteousness of his mounting the blue. A good horse bought with old Gilead's money, so he'd heard. Fitting and proper the animal should be at the end of the Gilead herd.

There were more than twenty men riding with him and ten more waiting at the camp. Ten men each would split up the beefs and move their share. And Ed Duncan would be riding ahead of the herd, picking up the delivery money. He liked the part. As he put the blue out of the small canyon and past the now-sluggish river, he doffed his hat in mock salute to the corpse floating somewhere in its bowels or beached farther down, caught somewhere on a rotting stump. The bones would be gleaming in the heat of the new summer sun.

The trail rode swift and familiar. Until Ed reached the last twisted part. Gilead had brought them around the fallen trees, woven back on one another, effectively blocking the trail. Horse and rider could easily weave around the slender trunks, ducking through the thick brush and cursing. Cattle would come head-on to the tangle and split, running wild through the brush and dividing the herd. Duncan cursed again.

Rocks tumbled across the faint path; trees resisted

being pulled by stout horses goaded by their riders. The riders were forced to dismount and tie their horses. Ed faced the sullen group and gave orders for them to clear out the trees. Faintly, well beyond the men, there was the sweet sound of cattle bellowing, money on the hoof. He drove the men to get the clearing done faster. Greed was pushing at him.

"To hell with this, I ain't no damned railroad crew. I signed to run beef, not cut this damned junk."

Brewer Jacobs, young, lean, whip-fast with a pistol, stood to wipe the sweat off his face and scowl at Duncan. The men behind him muttered their agreement, shifted feet in the rocks, and put down their inadequate tools. A man needed more than knives and an occasional hatchet to cut down a twisted pine.

"You listening to me, Duncan? This work's for damned yahoos. I ain't no swamper. Get us to those cattle, man, or forget the blasted goddamn day. I tell you I ain't cuttin' no wood for no man."

Jacobs's face was shiny red, dust running into muddy rivulets at his neck and along his collar. Large black stains circled his arms and lined the back of his fancy white-piped shirt. He sure didn't look like any woodchopper.

Duncan took the two slow steps that brought him in easy range. One hand went out to the lean outlaw, palm up, supplicating. Jacobs looked down at the hand and started to raise his eyes to meet Duncan's when the bullet went right through the third button of the satin shirt. Brewer Jacobs was dead before the echo came back to the stunned men. His body took a long and slow time settling back into the rocks, finally resting wedged into the half-chopped brush that had discouraged the reckless young man. One arm twitched, the back arched in reflex, and then the body settled firmly into the restricting pile.

The voice was low, but all the men heard its challenge. "Anyone else tired of chopping wood?" Avoiding the bloody corpse, they went back to the partially severed roots and stumps, the tangled rocks. Duncan picked up the shrunken body of Jacobs and tossed it to one side, knowing that its presence would finish what rebellion was left after the sudden shot. He expected no more trouble.

One mile farther down the trail, twelve men jumped at the unexpected shot, winced as the echo came tumbling through the rocks that were their cover. Eleven men looked to Joe. He listened intently, straining forward to pick up any more sound. Then he eased back with a brief shrug, shaking his head in warning. On edge, nervous from the shot's fatal reminder, the men turned their heads from side to side, widening their eyes to pick out something, anything that was unusual, that would explain the shot. There was nothing. Then they, too, sat back, nerved up but willing themselves to continue the silent wait.

At first dark Joe went to each man, touching four lightly, sending the rest without words back to the meager camp for a hard meal and a short sleep. He

would sleep later and be back on watch before the false-
ness of early dawn. This day had been the longest. This
day was the one Duncan should have taken. The cattle
were settled below, the men tired from the long weeks
of the gather, the ranchers still bickering about the
count. This should have been the day Duncan rode into
the trap.

Chapter 22

The murky gray predawn covered their movements,
but it did not muffle the sounds. Bits clanked against
teeth, saddles groaned and settled with riders' weight,
horses snorted at suspicious shapes, and men cursed too
loudly. In ten minutes Duncan's men were ready to ride.

He mounted the big blue and brought the horse to a
half rear. Heads turned, horses blew loudly, one sorrel
mare kicked out at a pushy neighbor, and the echo of
the hard slap on the broad rump almost started a rodeo.
Men and horses finally settled, and Duncan waved one
hand, letting the blue out by inches. Words weren't
needed as the men found the line and let their own
breath out slowly. Ahead were ten thousand beefs
waiting for them. A flash of money for each man, all the
whiskey and women a man could want, more than he
could use, would be theirs in a few days. Beat the hell
out of thirty dollars a month and found.

Joe drew back his head and slipped away from the
concealing boulder. He'd seen a flash of something, a
blur that could be a man on horseback. Way down the

trail, at the end of a switchback. The light gray dawn made him squeeze his eyes shut and wipe them hard. Then look again. There was something moving.

He hunched down and scurried to the next man in line, touched him briefly, held up five fingers, and waited. The man nodded once, then skittered away, bent over and drawn in, eager now to run his bit with the message and come back to his post. Joe whistled once, drawing in on a dry mouth, trying for a late owl. A poor imitation, but one that Track Williams recognized. The bald head came up quickly, sighted in on Joe; those five fingers came up again. Track nodded and turned away. The message was on its way down the far side of the ambush trail.

There was another quick glimpse of what could be a horse, more timeless minutes waiting, then a solid shape, a tall blue horse, a rider wide-shouldered and beefy. A line of riders followed close behind the big man, each horse touching the animal in front, sometimes nipping at the too-close flesh. Tails swished in the close quarters; one rider leaned back to slap the muzzle of a bronc resting on his mount's butt. Soft cursing, leather complaining against the constant shifting weight.

Jack Allen lowered his blond head and tilted it sideways to Joe. Joe shook his slightly, held out one finger, wagged it back and forth slowly. Jack smiled crookedly and wished he could put the damn rifle down and really get to that itchy spot in his back. By all rights it belonged to one of the men riding single-file down his line of vision. This was going to be a massacre.

Deliberately, almost in slow motion, Joe raised his rifle, sighted on a retreating back. He could see the end of the line now. If too many more riders passed him, it would mean that Duncan had reached the lip of the valley rim. Abruptly he stood up, spooking the two horses directly in front of him. He could not fire coldly.

"Duncan, that's far enough. Haul in, or you're dead."

Ed Duncan dropped from the blue and fired. A barrage of shots came immediately from both sides of the file; three of Duncan's men were down before they touched their own weapons. A too-eager Wall Blaisdell stood for a killing shot and died before he finished sighting down the barrel. Duncan's rifle was accurate.

The big man rolled across the rocky ground. Snug up against the fall wall, he fired again and again at the loose formation of boulders covering Joe's men. A high scream was a reward. Then a limp figure flopped down between two rocks and gurgled unintelligible sounds through a smashed face before dying, choking to death on the bright flow of blood.

Joe saw the blue horse go down, saw another horse jam up against the floundering animal, its rider clinging grimly to the horn. Ed Duncan appeared suddenly under the frantic horse's neck, rifle butt-end in his hand. One swing knocked the wounded rider from the saddle and Duncan pulled himself into the saddle, spurs already tearing at the panicked horse's sides, driving it up and over the staggered blue. Horse and rider disappeared down the steep side into Blackman's canyon.

A shot splintered rock beside Joe's face, sending a shard tearing into his cheek, stabbing a bright pain into one eye. He spun and shot in one motion, unable to sight. He recognized the grim face that went down under his lucky shot—Spence, the unlucky guard his first day into the camp.

A quick glance told him the score. The surprise was almost complete. The long line of men was broken. His own had suffered as well: Wall Blaisdell was dead, Track had a growing stain across his upper arm and was working his rifle left-handed. Utah's face carried long streaks of blood, and one man across the file sat too upright and too still against his rock.

The alley was flooded with groaning men, horses thrashing in shock and terror, and two men standing with raised arms, weapons down at their feet. There was only Ed Duncan left.

The blue was up, blood running from a furrow along the flat side of his jowl, but body and legs sound. Joe stepped onto the horse from the off side and gathered the reins as the horse bucked into a gallop, eager to get away from the loud racket and the heavy sweet smells. Joe leaned over the horn and guided the blue with his hands on the sweaty neck, reckless in the wild plunge down the banking.

Duncan's horse was slowing, the deep wound in its shoulder bleeding the animal dry. Even a beating with the rifle butt brought no more speed from the dying horse. Joe eased up the blue, watching. Ahead of him, way ahead, were men catching up horses, saddling excited broncs, ready to come down the long canyon graze in search of the gunfire.

He slowed down his thoughts, concentrating on the wide-shouldered man just ahead of him, who now stood with feet set apart on the ground, two steps from the floundering sorrel. The big man's head came up at the advancing steps of the blue. The questioning face broke into a smile as Ed Duncan recognized the rider.

"Guess that river didn't finish you after all. Should have known not to trust a drunk's word. But I figured the river would end anything Hardin started. You're a damned lucky son, you are. Me, I thought ole Joey Gilead was dead. Planned these days on that fact. You're a god-almighty one lucky son."

Joe listened to the words and was almost fooled, almost taken in by the incessant drone of the gibbering sounds. His feet slipped the stirrups just as the butt end of the rifle smacked the blue between the eyes, bringing the horse to his knees with a deep groan, dumping Joe at Duncan's feet. He rolled frantically, remembering the force of those weighted boots. And came up to stand not far from the man.

Duncan made no threatening move toward Joe, seeming almost to relax, and smile. Then the smile grew, and the big man spoke in a pleasant, almost friendly voice to Joe.

"Funny thing, I stand here long enough, keep you away from me, and those anxious do-gooding cowboys'll be riding up here all full of fire and righteousness. They'll find them a ghost, a wicked sinful ghost that stole from its own kin. And they'll see me, not a friend, but someone they know was on the right side. Now what do you think they'll do?

"Why, they'll listen to me say something about the bloody ambush you rode into up above, and how some of their friends died trying to keep you from getting to that herd. And they'll just naturally shoot you down when you protest and start spouting words. Then they'll find me a horse and let me ride. For I'll be the hero this time. And you, you poor sorry bastard, will do nothing. It ain't in you to just shoot me now, standing here. So you'll just wait for those riders to get here."

The splinter in Joe's left eye kept it shut, blinding him to that side. His head throbbed from the small bits of stone, making the words that came from the big man waver in front of him, echo inside his head, push at the pressure behind his eye. But he knew well enough what Duncan was saying, and the son of a bitch was right. He hadn't been able to pull the trigger back up on the hill, when he had the broad back lined in his sights.

But he could hear the horses, coming fast. Coming from the mouth of Blackman's canyon, coming up on his blind side. He knew Duncan could get away this one more time.

The wide grin grew into a leer; it drew all of Joe's attention. The obscene smile widened beyond the face, consuming the man, becoming the only thing Joe could get in focus. He squinted against the swollen eye, struggled to open it. Duncan stood there in front of him, rifle hanging loosely from one hand.

"You ain't going to shoot, Gilead. Why, that would be cold-blooded murder. One murder is enough for a man like you." Duncan laughed at the one-eyed man facing him.

The laughter stilled. Joe Gilead's left eye opened, and the blood-streaked center glowed a bright green. Both eyes focused on Ed Duncan, and Gilead's right hand came up, knuckles white around the handle of the gun. One finger drew back the trigger and released it. For once Ed Duncan had read his man wrong.

The big man lunged sideways while he lifted his rifle, and got it to hip level before the bullet entered his chest. Another shot went through the back of his head as he was spun around, and blew him apart. The body landed hard, rolled partway over, and was still.

Joe could feel the riders circling him before he could see them. A horse nudged up into his back, pushing him one step, then two steps forward, to send him to his knees by Duncan's body. A disembodied voice told him to be still, to wait there with his buddy while the rest of his crew were rounded up. A man stayed behind to guard Joe as the rest rode up the wide, torn-up path dug out from the sloping side of the canyon by the two fast-descending horses.

Joe thought of telling his guard that it was Duncan, not he, that was the one, the leader, they all sought and feared. But the brief and bitter violence of the past hour had exhausted him, drained him of the compulsion to explain. Track Williams, Utah Smith, even Jack Allen—one of the men left above would talk, would do all the explaining needed.

Joe sat quietly, with his head back, resting on the hardness of a cool and comforting rock. Both eyes were closed against the blood red light inside his head, and he sat almost motionless in the warming sun.

Chapter 23

"It's done, Mr. Gilead. All finished. We got all of them." Elissa Stratmeyer could barely hear the words over the shifting jingle of the harnessed team. The rider spoke hurriedly to Evan Gilead, who sat beside her on the plumped seat of the old buggy. A heavy leather bag sat between the old man's feet, and his hands played restlessly with the reins, splayed fingers stroking the oiled leather, separating and then bunching the thick lines.

She watched the grayed head nod, then felt the old man stiffen beside her at the rider's words. The hand spoke fast and low, sometimes backing up to repeat to the old man's questioning. Then the tired horse was backed around and gigged into a lope, aimed at the thin entrance of Blackman's canyon. Elissa leaned to put a hand on the slumped shoulders of the old man. A big hand covered hers for a moment, then she heard the soft words.

"Listen, girl, I got a story for you. A good 'un. The rustling's done, them thieves caught and wiped out. We set a trap, Joe and me. To the backside of Blackman's, on a trail few know about. Joe and them others, they sat

188

and waited with the bait, them cattle we gathered for the count. Too big a herd for most men to steal, but that Ed Duncan, he got big ideas. Full of himself Ed Duncan was."

As the team walked passed the entrance to the canyon, a guard lazily picked up a hand in salute. Elissa liked the immediate recognition the old man commanded. She turned her face back to watch his, her eyes diverted by the automatic skill of his hands on the reins, the response he demanded and got from the unmatched team.

"We took some damage; Wall Blaisdell and a ranny working for Dunning are dead. Two good men. And some wounded; nothing bad. But them rustlers is done and quit."

She watched the smile grow and the bent and twisted face, widening to a wild grin, cracking the lined skin at mouth and eyes.

"Seems Joe himself got to Duncan. Man faded off, left his own men right in the middle of the ambush. Joe went after him, right down that goddamned slide. Pardon, missy."

The buggy stopped with a clear view of the wide back wall of Blackman's, the churned swath that running horses had made still fresh in the sandy hillside.

"Joe almost came to a sorry end. Guards thought he was the outlaw, kept him at rifle point until Track set them straight. Wasn't no way to let anyone know Joe's part in this, feared that if too many folks knew, the bait would lose its flavor."

He turned on the seat and watched the face of the young woman beside him as he spoke the next words. "Brought you along for a good reason, missy. Been watching you with Joe. You got a look to you when he's near says you're taken with him. And I'm knowing he's that way about you. Both got the same look.

"But he won't stay. Told me so. Won't let go of that mistake. Figured if I brought you here, left you to tend to him, then you can work on his staying."

She listened, and a multitude of quick words came and went as she heard the speech. The thoughts were too fleeting and too new to be caught with sounds. She could only nod her agreement. Then she heard the words that frightened her.

"Tend to him? He's hurt. Where is he, where's Joe?' She could shake the old man for his complacent smile and the casual dismissal of his son's injuries.

"Just bunged up a bit, missy. Doc's here, working on the wounded, but figured you could do for Joe."

The team had stopped again, this time by the slanted remains of an old cabin. Elissa could see Joe, sitting up against a rock, head back, eyes shut. That was all she could see through the wetness that filmed her eyes.

She did not see the old man drop the leather bag to the ground near her, nor did she see him wheel the team around and head back to the canyon's mouth. On her knees in front of Joe, she released a cry that threatened to strangle her.

One eye opened to her. The other was swollen shut. A purple bruise spread across the side of his mouth. But she did not see the damage, she only saw his face lighten as he saw her, watched the slow smile come to him that lifted the tired set to his mouth.

Elissa leaned into the arm that came out to touch her, settled gently against the warm flesh of his side, and put her head into the hollow waiting just for her beneath his collarbone. The circling arm held her tight, the hand resting just below her breast.

She could feel his mouth touch her hair, then the sweet weight of his head came down to rest on hers. She shifted slightly, feeling a growing urge to be closer to him, to have more of his body. A hand moved in a small circle on her ribs, then pressed into her belly in a pulsing motion that focused all her attention on its gentle touch. He spoke her name just once, then all movement ceased and she could feel the length of his body sag beside her, the weight come on heavier to her side.

She had no idea of the time they were together. But she finally turned her head to look into his face and the rawness of the swollen eye brought back her good sense. She moved the hand from her lap, shifted her shoulders into the loosened grip of the arm, and eased herself away from the now-sleeping man.

On her knees she studied the face. Drawn too fine, gray under the reddish streaking and sun-browned color. There was a gentleness to the face now, an easing of the lines at mouth and eyes. She could love this man forever.

The leather bag was in easy reach, and she went to it.

The old man was smart; it contained a jug of water, soft cloths, a small bottle of whiskey, all of what she needed to care for his son. Those faded eyes might be old, but they missed little.

"Miss, nothing's changed. I ain't staying. This makes it worse." Elissa's hand stopped its gentle cleaning of the flesh around the damaged eye. She looked into the open green eye, saw the pain mirrored inside, and could only nod her assent. Then her hand resumed its work, wiping at the pus gathered at the inner corner of the damaged eye, patting the surface of the lid, dripping water gently underneath. She would have to leave the rest for the doctor's care.

The voice, and the words, shocked Elissa. "Miss, I need me a horse, right now. Hardin never showed. I want him. He'll run, and I want him for his part in this."

Panic quickened her response. "What about Hardin? Wasn't he here; wasn't he part of all this?"

"He was the traitor. He passed on all the plans that these ranchers made, after your pa fired Duncan. He quit working the gather last week, too drunk to stay on a horse. We didn't want to tell anyone, would have taken only one slip to lose Duncan and the rest."

Elissa's voice rose. "But, Lucy, she's gone to the ranch today. To pick up her things. We thought Hardin would be here, with the other ranchers and your father. Away from the ranch. She only wanted a few things and wanted to be certain Hardin wasn't there when she went to get them."

Her hands reached out to Joe as if in supplication. He

192

pushed them aside, gently, but demanding her obedi-
ence. His first steps were staggered, then he steaded
with a hand on her shoulder, and repeated his request.

"I need a horse. Hardin will kill her, miss. He's drunk
all the time now. He'll kill her. Got to get a horse." His
face was wild, his one eye searching the area, as if a
horse would be waiting for him, standing tied to a bush,
stirrups just right, rifle snugged beneath the near fender.

Elissa came up from her knees in full flight, hands
waving, skirt wrapping between her legs as she ran. She
went past Joe, cursing the hobbling material. There
were cowhands farther down the canyon, resting now,
standing and talking, horses ground-tied beside them,
heads down, half-asleep.

She yelled something. One man turned to the sound
and saw the wildly running woman, the slow-moving
man behind her. One man mounted his bay and put the
horse to a run, gradually picking up speed. The bay slid
to a stop in front of Elissa, and the young rider saluted.

"Ma'am, can I help?" She grabbed at the bridle,
hauling at the high-headed bay.

"Please help. We need a horse; I need your horse.
Right now, please." He could make no sense of her
words and stared at the young woman, wondering at the
red flush to her fair skin, the pale yellow of the loosening blond hair. He never saw the man come up
behind him, the man who reached for the boot loosely
balanced in the wide stirrup.

But he felt his foot shoved from its resting place,
knew he was going off the bay as his leg was pushed

away from the heavy fender of the carved saddle. The boy grabbed for the horn, grabbed for anything that would fight off this unexpected attack.

Joe shoved hard with both hands, and the cowhand was lifted from the saddle. Elissa clung to the bridle. Before the boy recovered, his horse with its new rider was gone. Stunned by the betrayal and embarrassed by his spill, he watched the brown rump disappear down the canyon trail to the plains beyond. He wanted to call out his anger, but after a quick glance sideways at the young woman he thought to rescue, he stayed silent. Her words flowed over him, soothing his bruises.

"Thank you so much. We needed that horse. It's all right, the horse will be brought back to you. I'm so sorry for your fall; let me help."

The soft sweetness of the voice eased him; the firm hand reaching down helped him stand. And his confusion was covered by the lovely smile and more thank yous. He agreed, she needed his horse and he was glad he could help her by giving it.

Elissa forgot the young man beside her immediately as she watched horse and rider go beyond the mouth and out across the endless grass. Lucy, dear Lucy, pregnant, just beginning to show, becoming awkward and more careful. And Hardin Fowler, the drunken, fearful husband, waiting in the small ranch house.

"Hurry, Joe. Hurry." The plea was mouthed in silence.

Chapter 24

There were no signs of anyone at Wagon Wheel. Weeds grew to her ankles in the small garden she had cleared earlier this spring. One of the top rails in the corral was down, and there were two horses waiting at the back of the barn, ribs sticking through their unshed winter coats. There was no sign of Hardin's flashy sorrel, and no sign of the faithful gray who had pulled her too many miles.

The borrowed chestnut mare and shiny buggy were out of place in the desolation. Black harness gleaming, long flaxen tail flowing free and clean, buggy wheels freshly painted—they were wrong here. Lucy Fowler dropped the carriage weight at the outside of the front wheel to secure the mare's quiet stand while she climbed laboriously out of the cramped seat. The pregnancy did not show beneath the heavy pleated skirt, yet her movements were slowed down, restricted by the tight band of the waist against her swelling flesh.

The first thing she became aware of in the house was the overpowering smell. Rotted food, filthy clothing, rusted tools, but even more was the closed smell of unwashed flesh and spilled whiskey. Nothing surprised her anymore about her husband, and she felt only a overwhelming relief that he was not here. This was no longer her home, and she was glad.

It was only a few things she wanted from this place: some clothing, two quilts she had worked on through the long Dakota winter, and two pieces of jewelry her mother had left her. The rest would stay with Hardin on the Wagon Wheel, their loss overshadowed by her freedom.

There was an old canvas bag under the bed, big enough for the three dresses, the wool cloak, and the quilts. The house closed in on her, the smell and the vivid memories urging her to hurry, to leave as soon as she could. The quilts were stuffed into the open bag, pulling apart some of the careful stitching, tearing at the fragile materials. The dresses were piled in on top, mangled by the haste. The house dulled her senses with panic. Lucy hurried to the small wooden box hidden carefully behind the kitchen stovepipe, hidden where Hardin would never look.

"That all you taking, gal? Surely there's more you be wanting. Like that fine chest your daddy sent over when we thought you was carrying again, and that big old mirror with the fancy painted gold framing. Too bad the glass got busted, but I did promise you a new glass. Don't you want that fancy frame no more? It's a real beauty."

Hardin's voice, whiskey-harsh, probed at her for the raw spots that would hurt the most. It was a talent of his she had learned to hate. But he couldn't be here; he wasn't in this house with her. Lucy turned around slowly.

"That's right, gal. It's good ole Hardin. Good enough for you when no one else would have you. Good ole Hardin willing to take on someone else's bastard brat.

But not good enough for you now. Bet you like living at the Gilead place; bet you're trying to pretend you did marry Hank. Gal, you ain't showing no sense, coming back here."

She could not look at him. She didn't need to see his face. If she closed her eyes, however tight, the puffy face appeared before her, painted inside her eyelids. The blond hair thinning and ragged, the red lines of his nose and cheeks, soft flesh blunting the once-pretty lines of him.

A hand touched her hair, forced her chin up, waggled her head back and forth as if demanding her attention. Lucy obliged him for a moment and then lowered her head again and tucked back, retreating from his touch, pulling her face from his cupped hand.

But the voice would not leave her. "You're still mine, Lucy. Mine. No one else's. There ain't no one else for you, gal. Hank's been dead nine years now. And that fancy brother of his is dead, too. I seen you watching that boy, knew you would figure if ole Hank wouldn't take you, then the baby of the family would do. Anything to become a respectable Gilead."

Words were useless; denial would only bring on more jeering taunts, more gloating laughter at whatever she said. Lucy tried to block out the sense of the words, willing herself to hear only the garbled sounds.

"What do you know. Nothing for our pretty little gal to say to her rightful husband. Them two brothers really took your fancy, didn't they, gal? And I killed both of them. Pretty slick; no one ever figured it out. I . . ."

The last of the words came through her panic. Lucy flinched at their meaning. Hardin killed both of them, both of the Gilead brothers. That fitted better than anything else. Hardin would laugh to see Joe Gilead suffer for the nine years. He would enjoy the pain. Finally her voice came out small and cracked, but the words were strong enough to stop Hardin's rambling insults.

"He was your friend, Hardin. Your only friend. Why would you kill your friend?"

"Hell and be damned, gal. He had everything I wanted, and gave me shit all. Including you. Now I got you, and I got this ranch, and now my share of them ten thousand beefs. Going to get your daddy's spread, going to be the man in these parts from now on. Old Gilead's gone to hell; the rest of them is nothing. Cattle all took and sold, and the cash'll be in my pockets.

"It's me now, gal. Me that's going to be the big one around here. Me, and you be damned with the rest of them."

Why was he telling her all this; why would he confess with such pleasure to someone who hated him so? Lucy shied away from what she did not want to face. Then Hardin's hand came out to squeeze her enlarged breast, twisting to hurt, mocking a gesture that could mean love.

"One more time, little gal. One more time. You be growing bigger titties now, more like a woman than the scarecrow I been living with too long now. I like titties like this. One more time, and then it's done for you. All done and finished.

"I'm moving on, gal. Figure to take up with that pretty blonde one been siding up to the old man, hoping to pick up the rest of the Three V for her pa. But I'll have me one more time with you."

She tried to turn away, but the hand twisted harder, drawing unwilling tears from her, ending her attempted flight. She could only stand where Hardin wanted her, right before him, head bent, body compliant.

"You know where to go. You know the way to our marriage bed. That nice high bed where we spent the last eight years. This one more time I'll take my pleasure there. You do just what I tell you."

The dark room was close, stuffy, the bedding tumbled and twisted, dust thick on the one battered table under the small window. Something rolled under her foot as she crossed the floor to the high standing bed, and a quick-darting shape across the corner of the room added to her fright. Hardin was right behind her, shoving her forward, hand at the small of her back. The final push sent her sprawling facedown on the stiff horsehair mattress.

Her eyes flicked from side to side, but there was nothing she could see within her reach that would help. Just this one more time. She could hear Hardin fumbling with his clothing, the sounds just behind her head, but she could do nothing more than wait.

One hand pushed at her, rolled her in the smelly bedding. The other hand tore at her clothing, pulled at her skirt, raised it over her head, shutting out the leering face.

"You getting prettier now, Lucy gal. More flesh to you. Seems almost a shame to give this up. But there's better waiting for me. Lots better."

The hand stroked her exposed belly, cupped the mounded softness above the dark hair. She was thankful he did not know a child was inside her, under his stroking hand.

"Hardin." The voice was clear, the command strong. "Get out here, Hardin."

Lucy felt the weight move off her, could sense Hardin stand for a moment, then walk from the room. For a long time she lay on the smelly bed and did not want to know what was happening outside the door.

Hardin knew the voice. For one sharp moment of panic he believed a ghost had come back to claim him. Joe Gilead's ghost. Who had to be dead, who was floating somewhere in the twisted bed of the Little Missouri, weighted down by a back full of buckshot.

"Hardin, I'm waiting for you. Take your time, Hardin. I'm giving you the chance you didn't give me. Outside. I'm waiting for you outside."

If a ghost were truly waiting for him outside, he damned well would take his time in getting there and would pick himself up a weapon to protect himself. "Coming, Joe. Coming right out real peaceable. Been wanting to talk to you; want my chance to explain. Coming right out there, Joe." He slipped a knife into his sleeve and picked up a pistol from a table where he'd dumped it too many days ago. Better than having

200

nothing in his hands when he faced the ghost.

But ghosts didn't come back with new blood streaking their face. Hardin started when he saw the swollen eye, the clean and untorn shirt. The real Joe Gilead for damned sure. Relief weakened him for a moment, then he stiffened. No one but a fool believed in ghosts.

"Thanks be to God, Joey. You're alive. I thought you was Duncan, found out the son was selling us out. That's why I waited for him, took that shot . . ."

"Don't bother, Hardin. It's all done. Duncan's dead, the herd still in Blackman, nice and safe. I came for Lucy. You let her go, and then we'll settle."

Hardin saw a chance. "So that's why you killed your own brother, wanted his woman. Never would have figured you for that, Joey." He wanted to grin when he saw the flash burn in Joe's eyes. One of the eyes was red and sore-looking, but it opened just enough in the flare of temper for Hardin to know the words had hit their mark.

The anger died a quick death, and the face before him stilled. One hand came up in a gesture of command, and there wasn't a tremor in the lean body.

"Send Lucy out, Hardin. The whole valley knows your part in this. Give me Lucy, and I'll let you go. It's for your life now, Hardin, and I'm giving it back to you."

The two men were only steps apart. Fowler swayed, off balance from the shock of Joe's presence, tilted from the steady drinking and the death of his plans. He

201

glared at the younger, stronger man, hatred drawing the remains of his handsome face into a caricature of his youth.

Joe watched for the sudden move. He could not bring this man back to Resolution, alive or dead. He could not turn him over to Blaine Hardesty. He had been a part of his growing up, a big part of his brother; to Joe this was a debt he had to clear. As long as he knew Lucy was safe, he would let Hardin run.

And he knew Hardin would take the chance, would run blind from his ranch, his wife, seizing the chance to flee his mistakes and his greed. Pity clouded Joe's instincts for a brief moment; Hardin Fowler could never run away from himself.

Fowler went for the pistol stuck in his pocket. It came out easily and pointed a bitter mocking finger at Joe. With no further thought, Fowler pulled the trigger, the barrel aimed at Joe's chest, less than five feet away.

The short gun misfired; it clicked hard and sharp in the stilled air. Hardin recocked the pistol and fired again. Joe slammed into Hardin as he jerked the trigger the second time, and the bullet shot wild over their heads. The noise brought Lucy from her half sleep on the musty bed; she sat up, frightened in the closed room.

Hardin fought dirty; he knew no other way. He raked the pistol across Joe's face, aiming for the eyes and at the same time brought his knee up to Joe's groin.

Hands twisted against each other, muscles strained, as

each man fought to control the gun. The barrel dug deeply into Joe's belly, and he could hear the hammer click as Hardin pulled it back. He tore at Hardin's wrist and deflected the next bullet's course. The hot blast burned across his arm, and the bullet richocheted off the roof.

Hardin dropped the gun, sending Joe off balance. The knife slipped from Hardin's sleeve into his hand in one smooth motion. His lungs gasped for air, his body shaking from the unnatural exertion, sending up a message craving whiskey. Hardin gauged the distance between himself and his foe, took two steps, and brought the knife out into the light.

"Joe, look out. He's got a knife." The words came almost too late. Lucy stood at the top step, eyes wide as the knife magically appeared. Hardin went at Joe's blind side, the knife ready to slip into soft flesh.

Joe slammed into the man, driving him back against the bottom step with his fury. He could feel the raw edge of the steps dig into old wounds in his back as they rolled and bounced from the step. Hardin's right hand held the knife; the two men rolled together, going over twice before Hardin's weight told and he straddled Joe, one knee holding an arm, one hand around his neck.

He drove the knife at Joe's throat. His weight shifted, and Joe slid underneath him. The knife continued its arc and sliced thinly through Joe's shirt, pinning him to the ground. Hardin grabbed for the impaled blade, and Joe rolled from under him. They both grabbed for the handle, Hardin's hand reaching first. Joe pinned the knife between their bodies and slammed his weight into the softer man.

But it was his own weight that drove the knife into him. Hardin groaned with the bitter pain. The fight ended as quickly as it had started. Hardin's sigh, his abrupt ending of the struggle, told Joe what had happened.

Joe rolled from the body underneath him, rolled to lie flat on the warm, giving ground. He rested a moment beside the still-breathing corpse. He could look over at the man and see death drain the florid face. He could see the handle of the rusted knife sticking from Hardin's exposed belly, the blood welling slowly, continually, from around the dulled blade.

Hardin Fowler was still alive. The pain had not yet started on him yet, but there was no chance for him to live. His eyes opened, and one hand twitched in the dirt, rising for a fluttering moment to pass near the protruding handle.

Joe lay beside him, panting from the battle, his head was inches from Hardin's, and he could watch as the waves of nausea started, as the pain began from the belly wound. It took a long time, but Hardin's eyes finally found Joe's face, finally looked at him clearly, hate still muddying the clarity of the blue eyes.

Fowler tried to speak. Opened his eyes and worked his mouth slowly, drawing in air, making low, guttural noises, but no words came. Lucy did not go to her husband; she sat on the bottom step, her feet just in back of

Joe's head. Joe tried to sit up, but the effort wasn't worth it.

He lay back in the dirt and watched Hardin Fowler die. Lucy remained on the bottom step, quiet, dry-eyed, her face streaked with dust, her dress torn, the skirt just covering her knees. She listened to the gasping sounds, the harsh rattle, and then sat in the blessed silence.

She had something for Joe Gilead, a present for him. The words spoken by Hardin, when he thought she would die with the knowledge. That it was Hardin and not Joe who had been the killer nine years ago. The words sounded in her head and let her smile at the green-eyed man who lay quiet in the dust. She would tell him soon enough.

Epilogue

Elissa was the first to reach the small ranch. Back in Blackman's canyon another grinning young cowhand was minus a horse. The unmatched team caught up to her an hour later, driven by the old man, with a tall, unbending passenger in the seat beside him.

The team stopped of its own accord, Evan Gilead's hands slack on the reins. A body lay at the bottom of the steps, and the dark stain surrounding it could be nothing but blood. A towel had been put over the features, but the form of Hardin Fowler was unmistakable.

On the top of the steps sat two women, one older and worn, her skirt pinned together along one side, a dark-ening bruise on her neck. The other woman was

205

younger, eyes shining, long hair free-flowing. The two conversed in soft and easy tones and barely looked up as the team brought the two men into the yard.

Another body lay stretched out along the veranda, wrapped with a rakish strip of white sheeting across the left side of his face. The sight quickened the old man's heart, shortened his breath, brought a fear to him that almost made him cry out.

Until he saw a hand lift slowly from the long body, a hand that waved in the direction of the team and buggy. A voice followed, a voice that eased the old man back in the seat with relief.

"How do, Pa. Visit with you later. Got to do some serious catching up on my sleep." The hand settled slowly on the torn shirt, just above the beltless jeans that were gray with dust.

Joe's voice, Joe's old humor, that would let him tease in the middle of a storm. Elissa smiled at the old man. Her face let him know that all was settled, and his son was back for good.

Center Point Publishing

600 Brooks Road • PO Box 1
Thorndike ME 04986-0001 USA

(207) 568-3717

US & Canada:
1 800 929-9108